Dear Reader,

It's true. A woman never forgets her first time.

Although I'd written several earlier novels, *Stormy Courtship* was my first Harlequin Temptation title. And the beginning of a professional relationship that's now in its second decade.

This is a story of one woman's quest to prove the innocence of the man she loves—a man who follows his conscience, even when his actions put his reputation in jeopardy. It also explores my favorite themes of love, honor and family.

I do hope you enjoy Dan and Jonnie's love story.

JoAnn Ross

JoAnn Ross

STORMY
COURTSHIP

MIRA BOOKS

MIRA

ISBN 1-55166-072-5

STORMY COURTSHIP

Copyright © 1985 by JoAnn Ross.

All rights reserved. Except for use in any review, the reproduction or utilization of this work in whole or in part in any form by any electronic, mechanical or other means, now known or hereafter invented, including xerography, photocopying and recording, or in any information storage or retrieval system, is forbidden without the written permission of the publisher, MIRA Books, 225 Duncan Mill Road, Don Mills, Ontario, Canada M3B 3K9.

All characters in this book have no existence outside the imagination of the author and have no relation whatsoever to anyone bearing the same name or names. They are not even distantly inspired by any individual known or unknown to the author, and all incidents are pure invention.

MIRA and the star colophon are trademarks of MIRA Books.

Printed in U.S.A.

To Steven Axelrod,
whose belief in this story kept
me writing through the hard times

Chapter One

Jonnie Ryan's skirt swirled about her knees as she executed a stiff turn in the narrow hallway and began pacing in the opposite direction. She'd been wearing this path in the bark-colored vinyl flooring for thirty-five minutes and was beginning to wonder just how long Dan Kincade was going to play his little game. This visit had been her idea—not his, and Dan seemed to be making it clear that she hadn't been invited to his office today.

In fact, she considered, stopping for a moment in front of the trophy case, if this were medieval times, Dan would probably have hauled up his drawbridge and sent his guards to pour boiling oil down on her. Civilization being what it was, he was forced to employ more subtle means of warfare. And keeping the new investigator for Oregon's state commission on

collegiate athletics cooling her high heels in the hallway would have to do.

The trophies spanned several decades, some of the
older ones dating from her father's time here at the
College of the Cascades. Jonnie thought how ironic it
was that she'd found herself, after all these years, back
here—thrown together with Dan Kincade again. She
shook her head, her auburn hair fanning out in a soft,
fiery cloud. Her oval face took on a stern expression.
It was done and done with long ago. She was a grown
woman now, with a law degree on her wall and a
brand-new political appointment that could boost her
career several notches. She wasn't about to allow her
past folly as an overly romantic young girl to stand in
her way.

The door opened, and a young woman came out.
She was obviously a coed, and Jonnie reflected that
her position as secretary to the head basketball coach
was probably quite a plum. She wouldn't be at all
surprised if there was a waiting list in the student em-
ployment offices.

"Coach Kincade will see you now." The dark-haired
girl smiled at Jonnie. "I'm sorry you had to wait, but
he had all this—" She nodded at the stack of manila
folders she clutched against her sweater.

"That's all right," Jonnie assured her. "I understand." *More than you'll ever know,* she added silently. She took a deep breath, squared her shoulders
and entered the room.

Dan Kincade was leafing through a stack of papers, but he looked up as she entered. Jonnie was struck, not for the first time, by the vivid contrast between his curly, jet-black hair and crystal-blue eyes. He stood up immediately, coming around the desk to greet her.

"Smile," he commanded by way of greeting, enclosing her hand in both of his.

Jonnie had imagined this interview many times. She'd honed it, edited it, altered it a thousand different ways until she'd gotten it to a point where she felt in control of the conversation. But she'd never expected him to begin it in such an unorthodox fashion. And she certainly hadn't counted on the jolt to her senses imparted by the long fingers that closed over hers.

"Why?"

"I want to see if your father got his money's worth."

At the teasing grin, lifting the corners of Dan's mouth, Jonnie smiled, a wide friendly smile that displayed perfectly straight teeth.

"Beautiful." He nodded his approval. "And worth every penny."

He gestured toward a chair in front of his desk, and Jonnie complied, crossing her long legs with a smooth gesture that did not go unnoticed by Dan's vivid blue eyes. She tugged the emerald silk over her knees and forced herself to meet his candid assessment.

Dan lowered his tall body into the leather chair behind the desk, making a tent with his fingers as he rested his elbows on the wooden arms. He swiveled slowly, side to side, studying her.

"It's good to see you, Jonnie."

His deep voice held a smile, and Jonnie wondered what had ever made her think she could face this man without suffering a vivid reminder of the last time she'd talked to him. She only hoped he'd forgotten that day. After all, she undoubtedly hadn't been the first girl to throw herself at him. And considering the fact that he was, fifteen years later, even better-looking, she couldn't have been the last.

"You've changed," he noted unnecessarily, his eyes paying silent compliments as they moved from the top of her wavy auburn hair down her figure, which looked custom-tailored for her five-foot, ten-inch frame. Those eyes moved along the firm, shapely curve of her calf to her slim ankles, returning slowly to her sea-green eyes. "All grown up."

"As opposed to that skinny kid with the mile of railroad tracks running across her teeth?" Jonnie returned dryly. "It would stand to reason I've changed, Dan. We can't remain teenagers forever, thank God."

"That'd be the pits, wouldn't it?" he agreed with a friendly grimace. "I've already noted the braces did their job admirably, but let me point out I never had any doubts that the skinny kid would blossom into quite an attractive woman."

Jonnie felt a stab of pain as she remembered how she'd appeared in those days. All her energy had gone into shooting her body upward, without giving any thought to those proportions that mean so much to a teenage girl. Not to mention teenage boys. She'd been too tall, too gangly. What had ever possessed her to think she could attract that all-star collegiate hero?

She experienced a warmth of admittedly feminine satisfaction that Dan now found her appealing. But Jonnie shook it off, knowing if she allowed the lingering remnants of a schoolgirl crush to interfere with her job, it could only prove disastrous.

"I hadn't realized you'd given it any thought," she admitted. With the twenty-twenty vision of hindsight, Jonnie had accepted long ago that Dan Kincade could not have been expected to notice a skinny thirteen-year-old girl.

"Of course," he answered simply. "You reminded me of my kid sister. She was a stringbean, too. But by the time she was eighteen, she had a figure that had men walking into walls." He grinned, his blue eyes twinkling. "You were, as I recall, just in too much of a hurry to grow up."

A tiny flush appeared high on her cheekbones as Jonnie recalled all too vividly the humiliation she'd suffered. The soft rose color caught his attention.

"You've lost your freckles," he said, shaking his head with what appeared to be honest regard. "I always liked them."

It was one of those mysteries of nature that the scattering of freckles that had given Jonnie such grief in her adolescent years were now represented by only a small sprinkling across the bridge of her nose. The others, oddly enough, seemed to have fallen, as if toppled by the forces of gravity to grace her shoulders. A few light ones were scattered along the curve of her breasts.

Jonnie answered before she could give adequate thought to her words. "Not lost. They've moved."

Whatever else had changed in her life, Dan Kincade proved he hadn't. The devilish gleam in his eyes demonstrated he was just as receptive to a woman's charms as he'd been in his undergraduate days.

"Interesting." His gaze moved with some horrid psychic power to the bodice of the emerald silk dress. "I'd like to see them again someday. For old-times' sake."

Her answering gaze turned brittle as Jonnie realized Dan was not above attempting to use her past feelings for him as an obstacle to her performing her duty.

"I'm sure you know why I'm here, Dan," she sad, folding her hands in her lap. Only the slight, unconscious swinging motion of her crossed leg displayed her discomfort with their situation.

"Of course I do. And I've got a question about that."

Jonnie arched a russet brow, encouraging his inquiry.

"Does your father know what you're up to these days?"

Her eyes widened with surprise. "Of course he does. Why wouldn't he?"

Dan refrained from answering immediately, shrugging wide shoulders as he began doodling absently on a yellow legal pad. His eyes, when they lifted back to her face, were faintly censorious.

"I wouldn't have thought, after all basketball has meant to him, that you'd want him to know what you're doing to ruin the sport."

"I don't understand how you can say that." Jonnie's fingernails dug into her skin as she squeezed her hands together more tightly. "Dad has always fought to keep the game clean," she argued. "Besides, as you pointed out, Dan, I'm quite grown up now. I make my own decisions." Her words were bitten off, one at a time, as she met his gaze.

"I hope they're not all as bad as this one," he muttered. Then, once again demonstrating his uncanny ability to throw her off the track, he smiled.

"How is your father? I haven't seen him in far too many years."

"Dad's fine," Jonnie answered distractedly, attempting to reorganize her rehearsed interview. She was determined to gain control of this seesaw conversation.

"He's done great things as athletic director down at Shasta State. I was surprised to read he was stepping down."

Jonnie laughed, drawn away from her good intentions once again. "You know Dad. He swears every year he's going to retire and go fishing. But can you honestly see that man sitting still long enough to hook any kind of fish? You basketball coaches are just one mass of kinetic energy."

She grinned, shaking her head in mock frustration. "It was hard enough to get him off the court. They'd have to use blasting powder to get him out of the AD's office."

Dan shared her laughter, his memories of Tom Ryan as warm as her own. "That man lives and breathes the sport, that's for sure. I remember the time he told me heaven was going to be a lot like the NBA, but without the twenty-four-second time clock."

"That sounds like dad," she agreed. "He once told me that the original Boston Celtic's Dutch Dehnert was visited by the ghost of James Naismith. Instead of being frightened, Dutch wanted to know if they played basketball in heaven."

"I remember that story," Dan broke in with a grin. "And James said, 'Dutch, I've got good news and bad news. The good news is they do.'"

"'The bad news,'" Jonnie finished the often-told tale, "'is that you're starting tomorrow.'"

Their shared laughter eased the tension that had been building in the room. Dan's face softened as he absently tapped the pencil on the pad.

"You know, your dad taught me a lot about the game. But he taught me even more about life, Jonnie.

I was one scared kid when I showed up to play ball here. Being a prep-school jock and playing college ball at one of the nation's top-ranked schools were two entirely different things."

"You certainly never showed you were scared by the way you played," she stated, granting him that. *On or off the court,* she tacked on silently.

Despite his reputation as a heart breaker, Jonnie couldn't deny that Dan had been an exceptional talent. He'd been recruited personally by her father during his years as head coach here. Tom Ryan's sharp eyes had caught a quality in Dan he'd sworn would take the kid far. Which it had. After a brilliant college career, followed by an equally rewarding time in the NBA, Dan was now head coach at the College of the Cascades.

"He gave me a lot of confidence when I needed it badly," Dan remembered. "Later, he helped me keep everything in perspective. He always said winning wasn't everything; it was improvement that counted. He reminded me that I should never be satisfied and always try to do better. You know, I still remind myself of that every morning."

"I know," Jonnie said softly. "I got the same sermon."

"Did it take?"

A smile touched her face. "It took," she confirmed.

Jonnie recalled how her father always considered Dan Kincade special. Perhaps that had been another reason, besides Dan's skill on the court, his easy humor and his exceptional good looks, that Jonnie had developed such a crush on him. Her father's approval had meant a lot to her in those days. And despite her assertion that she was an adult, capable of making her own decisions, she'd have to admit it still did.

She'd grown up in a motherless household, but Tom Ryan had managed, despite his hectic career, to be both mother and father to Jonnie. Although there'd admittedly been times she missed the feminine companionship a mother could have offered, there had never been anything she couldn't go to her father with. Including that ridiculous episode with Dan.

"Well, here you are," Jonnie said briskly, returning the conversation to the present, "in his position now. Let's just hope you're living up to everything he taught you."

Dan's eyes narrowed, a steely cast darkening the blue. "I suppose we're back to the commission," he remarked flatly.

"That's why I'm here, Dan. Not to hash over old memories."

He stood up, combing his long fingers through his thick jet curls. "Of course I'm willing to cooperate with you, since I've obviously got no choice. But respect and affection for Tom keeps me from telling you precisely what I think of your Murdock Commission's witch-hunt."

Jonnie was on her feet in an instant, glaring up at him. At her height, especially wearing high heels as she was today, it was an odd sensation to have to look up to meet a man's eyes. It put her at a distinct psychological disadvantage.

"This isn't a witch-hunt. And I resent you calling it that."

"Well, whatever it is," Dan stated with almost bored resignation, as he moved toward the office door, "it'll just have to wait until after practice."

"Practice?" Jonnie slammed her purse down onto the desk, finally losing patience. "You're the one who insisted on five o'clock this afternoon. You're the one who kept me waiting outside this office door for over half an hour. And you're the one who conveniently neglected to mention you'd scheduled practice. I suggest, Dan, you try fitting your timetable to my schedule this time. I'm ready to go over your figures."

Dan folded his arms and looked down at her, his even gaze daring Jonnie to do anything about this latest delaying tactic.

"Gotta have a practice, Jonnie," he replied simply, ignoring her outburst. "You can't expect the Lumberjacks to keep up the old winning tradition established by daddy without one."

"Then you should have made our appointment for this morning."

"I was busy this morning."

"Well, I was busy this afternoon, but I came," she argued. "Just what am I supposed to do while you're conducting practice?"

Dan shrugged carelessly. "I don't know. I suppose you can come watch. Maybe even give me a few pointers. As I recall, you played pretty well yourself. For a girl."

He was doing it again. Baiting her. Manipulating everything so he'd be the one in control. Jonnie knew it, but at this point she didn't know exactly what she could do about it. If she stomped out, as she'd dearly love to do, she'd only end up wasting the day. If she trailed after him, sitting around while he ran his damn practice, at least she'd be able to meet with him afterward, salvaging something from her efforts. She sighed, giving up the battle.

"All right," she agreed. "But afterward we need to get down to work."

"Sure," he agreed, putting his hand under her elbow as he led her out the door and down the long hallway.

He needn't have directed her. Jonnie remembered the way as if she'd walked these corridors yesterday. A series of tunnels connected the massive structure of Ryan Coliseum, named for her father, with the athletic department offices. She liked the way Dan's stride matched her own. She was used to that with her father and her brothers, but the rest of the time it seemed she was always having to shorten her gait to baby steps when walking with others.

As they entered the cavernous interior of the building, a flood of old memories washed over her. She stood in the doorway eyeing the tiers of bleachers, the highly polished wooden parquet flooring and an electronic scoreboard that hadn't existed during her father's tenure.

"Bring back memories?" Dan asked softly, his tone much warmer than it had been moments before.

Jonnie looked up and watched his eyes warm with affection as they moved across her face. She'd seen that look before—the day when, with all the fervor of a thirteen-year-old wildly in love, she'd professed her feelings.

Dan had taken her gift and treated it tenderly. She admitted this years later, although it hadn't seemed so at the time. He told her she was far too young to be thinking about love and marriage and that she'd have plenty of time when she was grown up.

"You're a terrific kid, Jonnie." Dan had done his best to assure her. "You're a great sport and a heck of a little ballplayer." He bent, kissing her cheek lightly. "And I've not a single doubt that when the time is right, you'll make some guy a terrific wife. Give it time, honey."

After that he had left, and Jonnie ran home to cry buckets of devastated tears into her pillow.

It was disconcerting, knowing she and Dan were sharing the same memory. Jonnie decided they had done enough reminiscing.

"Not really," she answered his question, unwilling to meet his gaze as she started walking toward the bleachers at the far end of the court. "But then again,

I've been in so many gyms in my life, it's difficult to tell them apart.''

"I can imagine," Dan said. Gently persuasive, he took her arm and effectively turned her in the opposite direction. "Come see what you think of this year's crop."

Jonnie realized she wasn't going to get away with hiding up in the top bleachers. For some unfathomable reason he was going to make her sit beside him through this practice. If she were to protest, she'd only appear foolish and allow Dan to see how much this entire incident was beginning to unnerve her.

She watched with reluctant admiration as he ran the team through the scrimmage. He paced the sidelines, his hands jammed into the pockets of his gray dress slacks, radiating all the intensity of a caged panther. If this was the energy the man generated for a mere practice, Jonnie wondered what he'd be like in a game. She knew basketball coaches were some of the most volatile men in sports, but Dan seemed determined to surpass even the most exaggerated of reputations. His whistle blew with a continual shrill outburst as he repeatedly made substitutions.

"Richardson!" The deep voice bellowed a harsh warning to a guard who had just sent his huge frame flying into another player who had set his position.

"Kid lived and died by blocking shots in high school," Dan informed her as he halted his sideline march for a minute, his eyes still directed on the action. "Now all we have to do is teach him to shoot, rebound and think. And make certain he manages to get an education. All in four years. Should be a cinch, right?''

He was off again, his long finger pointing at a player who'd just missed a flamboyant attempt at a free-wheeling dunk shot.

''Jackson! What's the eleventh commandment around here?''

The entire team answered in unison, not stopping their fast break down the court. ''Thou shalt not miss a dunk!''

''I seem to remember you missing a few,'' Jonnie murmured under her breath as he passed.

Dan skidded to a halt, the surprised expression on his face slowly evolving into a wide grin. ''Shhh.'' He placed a finger over his lips as he turned his attention away from the practice. ''Twelfth commandment—the coach is always right. We don't talk about my near misses around here. And if you're referring to that time in the NIT finals when I took off from the foul line and came up short, lady, remember I was skilled enough to get the rebound and do a backward dunk that effectively kept everyone off my back.'' His blue eyes twinkled attractively. ''Until now.''

''Skilled?'' Jonnie retorted lightly. ''You were *lucky* to get that rebound. Skill had nothing at all to do with it.''

''And here I had the wild idea you thought I was perfect back in those days.''

Jonnie found herself enjoying the easy bantering that had been so much a part of their relationship. Dan had been like one more big brother in a house filled with men. Until she'd been foolish enough to fall in love.

"Not perfect," she corrected. "Although I'll admit you weren't bad, Kincade. Who knows, with a little more practice, you may have been able to do those dunks right."

"It's only because I'm a great fan of your dad that I'm willing to forget you ever said that, Jonnie Ryan. But don't think for a moment you can get away with it all the time." He gave her a grin that sent tingles rushing all the way to her toes.

As abruptly as the exchange began, it was over. Dan turned his attention back to the scrimmage, barking out a few new instructions with a voice that would have done justice to the fiercest of bull mastiffs.

Finally, when the players looked ready to drop from exhaustion, Dan sent everyone from the floor—not to the showers, as Jonnie hoped, but into a training room.

"Game films." He answered her questioning gaze. "Last night's loss."

Jonnie wondered why Dan was altering the practice schedule this way. She knew the usual procedure was to show the films first, then work on the weak points. But since it was none of her concern, other than idle curiosity, she nodded, remaining silent.

The lights were cut, the silence punctuated by the whirring grind of the film running through the projector and the occasional groans from players forced to relive a less-than-successful moment. Dan straddled a chair he'd pulled up next to her, his arms resting across the top. From time to time he'd stop the action, drilling the young team on where they'd gone wrong. To be fair, Jonnie noted, he also halted the film to reward a good play.

So intent was Dan on the film that he appeared to have forgotten she existed. Under the cover of semidarkness, Jonnie felt freer to examine him. He was as appealing as ever, she decided. Even more so, with the handsomeness of his youth having matured the strong features of a ruggedly attractive man. His jet-black curls seemed thicker, and she noticed he was wearing his hair a little longer these days. Those incredible blue eyes were still lashed with a sumptuous black fringe. The line of his strong nose was not as straight nor as smooth as it had once been. Too many elbows had made their mark, adding a roughness to his features not there in his younger days.

For some reason, the idea of Dan suffering the pain that was an accepted part of his profession caused Jonnie to shiver with an odd sense of dread. The cleft in his square chin had deepened, and just above it his lips were as full as she remembered them, almost voluptuous. When you took each of Dan Kincade's features individually, they appeared to be almost too pretty to belong to a man. But when you set them all into his rugged face, Dan was undoubtedly all male.

"Okay, Ryan." He startled her, his low voice slicing into her thoughts unexpectedly as he put the action on freeze-frame. "From what you've seen so far—from the practice and the game film—what would you do?"

He'd only murmured the question; it had gone unnoticed by the team and assistant coaches, but Jonnie could only stare at him in mute shock. What in the world was he asking her for? His pupils were black pools, widened in the dim light of the room, but in them she detected a sparkling challenge.

"What are you asking me for, Dan? You're the coach."

"I've got a hunch about something," he answered simply. "I'd like to check it out. Humor me—what would you do?"

His finger hadn't left the switch, and Jonnie realized he was willing to keep the film stopped until she responded to his out-of-the-blue request.

"Well . . . of course there's the obvious," she answered slowly, giving the matter some serious thought. "You've got yourself a fast team here, from what I've seen. And every one of them can pass and shoot . . . except Richardson," she added, remembering the bricks tossed up far short of the basket.

Dan nodded, rubbing his jaw as he waited for her to elaborate on her cautious evaluation.

Encouraged, Jonnie continued. "I'd try neutralizing the trap by sending your shooters in for layups and short jumpers. You don't have a real big team this year and it's going to be tough any time you come up against a muscle opponent. But a team like that is bound to be slower. I'd counter with my speed."

"Exactly what I'd planned to do." Dan's tone indicated pleasure with her analysis of the situation. "I knew under all that stiff, polished officialdom, you were still Tom Ryan's little girl."

Jonnie didn't know whether to be pleased that he'd agreed with her opinion, or irritated because he still hadn't fully acknowledged the fact that she was now a grown woman with a career. Talk about backhanded compliments! Suddenly the lights flooded the room and Dan allowed his team to escape.

"Ready to go to work?" he asked, climbing off the chair.

"That's what I'm here for," she agreed primly, walking back with him through the tunnel to his office.

"Have a seat," Dan invited. "I just need to finish up a few details."

Jonnie nodded, waiting quietly as he leafed through a stack of papers, jotting down information. Her gaze circled the room, taking in the photographs of Lumberjack players from years past. Many had gone on to fine careers in the professional ranks, and she felt a small glimmer of reflected pride in that knowledge. When her father had arrived at the small Oregon college, its basketball program had been nonexistent. But the regents had cleverly surmised that their sports future lay in basketball, rather than football. While a team of over forty players was necessary for football, basketball only required eleven to make up the starters and the second team. In a school with no aspirations to be anything but a small, well-respected liberal arts college, basketball was a natural. The College of the Cascades disbanded their football program, putting their recruiting eggs into the white mesh basket. The move paid off royally. The Lumberjacks always finished in the Top Ten in the UPI and AP polls and were always a favorite in the National Invitational Tournament.

Her appraising eye lingered on a faded photo of Dan at age twenty, appearing to fly through the air, the pebbled ball palmed in his large hand. She moved her gaze to the man he was today. He was engrossed in work, making a series of phone calls that stretched on for what seemed forever. Jonnie's hopes for an early evening diminished as he reached into a drawer and extracted a small dictaphone, answering a request for his appearance at a high-school sports-award banquet.

She glanced down at her watch, surprised to discover it was well past eight. She'd been on the run all day, settling for an apple she'd grabbed from the vending machine in her office building. Her stomach was definitely sending signals, threatening to rumble if she didn't do something about it. She dug into her purse, coming up with a breath mint she popped into her mouth hoping it would appease those hobgoblins of hunger trying to make themselves known.

The furtive action caught Dan's attention, and his blue eyes focused on her in a thoughtful study.

"Food," he said suddenly. "Let's go get something to eat."

He was still at it. Jonnie was getting extremely tired of this artful dodger, and she rubbed a hand at the back of her neck.

"Work," she corrected firmly. "I'm still waiting for some cooperation here, Dan."

"And you'll get it," he replied, rising from behind the desk, "as soon as I eat. I'm not very cooperative when I'm starving, Jonnie. If you hadn't been so busy building your political career these past years, you'd have learned what most women pick up at their mothers' knees."

"And that is?"

"The male of the species is always more docile when fed."

"What about the female?" Jonnie countered.

Dan winked as he took down a sports jacket from the bent wooden rack. "Never met a female who could be trusted to be docile at any time," he answered flippantly. He eyed her slim figure in the silk dress. "Don't you have a coat?"

A warm front had moved into the state, bringing temperatures that belied the January date of the calendar. It had been exceptionally temperate when she'd started out this morning and Jonnie had left her coat in her office, never expecting to still be working this late. Still? She hadn't even started.

"No. I hadn't realized we'd be playing a night game." Her tone told him she knew exactly what he was doing. Dan had employed every stalling tactic known to man thus far and showed absolutely no sign of relenting.

He confirmed her diagnosis as he held out his jacket. "Here, put this on. It's not very fashionable, but it'll keep you warm until the heater starts working in the car."

"I'm fine, Dan." Jonnie ignored the outstretched jacket.

"You're fine now because you're in a heated office," he argued patiently. "It's drizzling again and I don't want to be responsible for you catching a cold."

She gave in, knowing how the damp night air of the Willamette Valley could chill through to the bone.

"That's very nice of you." She slipped her arms into the sleeves, feeling incredibly unglamorous as the gray tweed hung far below the tips of her rose-tinted fingernails. No matter how hard she tried, she just couldn't seem to escape her adolescent image.

"Not really." Dan turned off the lights. "It's in the interest of the team. I've the distinct impression you're going to be hanging around here for a while. If you catch a cold, you'll probably give it to all the guys. There you'd be—Typhoid Jonnie—a one-woman disaster to Cascade's athletic program."

His eyes hardened to cold steel as they moved across her face, displaying none of his earlier friendliness. "Not that you're not working toward that end anyway, Jonnie. I'd just like to keep plague out of the picture."

Chapter Two

Jonnie returned Dan's jacket as they entered the restaurant, noticing that his arrival was causing a little flurry of activity. She watched the waiter as he prepared a table off in a quiet, hidden corner and wondered just how many times Dan had shared this table with some other woman.

She shook her head, disturbed by the thought of Dan Kincade with another woman. Jonnie hastened to assure herself that this feeling was only because a girl never quite forgets her first love. The only reason the man was affecting her so strongly was because she was reliving adolescent fantasies. Jonnie reminded herself she was here to represent the Murdock Commission, to investigate misdeeds in collegiate sports, not to fawn over a man who probably received far too much feminine adulation already.

"I'm still surprised that our little Jonnie is now a hotshot lawyer," Dan murmured, his blue eyes skimming her face as if to reacquaint himself with this new image. "You've made quite a name for yourself. Law Review, the youngest prosecuting attorney in the county's history, appointment to the staff of the Attorney General's Criminal Bureau. And now chief field investigator for the Murdock Commission. Quite a lot of feathers in such a pretty cap."

"I'm surprised you kept such close tabs on me, Dan," she murmured, unfolding her white damask napkin and placing it in her lap. Jonnie tried to hide the flush of pleasure she received from the idea of Dan Kincade maintaining some degree of interest in her over the years.

"It's been difficult to live sixty-two miles from the state capital and not keep up with you in the papers. One gets the distinct impression you're a combination of Wonder Woman, Eleanor Roosevelt and Morgan Fairchild."

Jonnie thought she detected some mockery in his tone, a disapproval which was magnified by his next statement.

"Not quite the hotshot little guard Tom was grooming to break open women's basketball." He shook his head. "I even heard a nasty rumor you didn't play in college. Tom must've suffered a coronary from the little trick."

"It wasn't a trick. I didn't want to play ball, Dan. College athletics are too time-consuming. I had better things to do with myself."

"So I've read," he drawled, his eyes bright with devilish insinuation.

Jonnie's hackles rose. She'd long ago accepted the fact that she was a highly visible person, garnering more attention than some of her equally adept colleagues. Part of her fame came from being Tom Ryan's daughter in a state that would have nominated the man for sainthood. Along with that, it was inevitable that the press would focus upon those who worked on the fringes of politics, living and dying professionally by propitious appointments. But she knew it was not that fame he was referring to.

Dan Kincade was obviously tiptoeing around those occasional blind items placed in the gossip columns of politically hostile newspapers to undermine her popularity and power base.

"You haven't exactly been bereft of fame yourself, Dan. And in case you hadn't noticed, there's not a lot of call for women in pro ball." Jonnie's voice was acidly combative.

"True." He surprised her by agreeing easily. "But there's always high-school or collegiate coaching."

Jonnie braced her elbows on the table, cupping her chin in her palms as she eyed him across the table. "Gee," she drawled with feigned sweetness, "aren't you generous? Offering to let me coach other women who'll have no chance to earn even a substandard living at something you men get superbucks for doing."

A shadow crossed Dan's face. "Are you that angry at me? Because I'm a man?" he asked gravely. "You know, Jonnie, if the situation were reversed, I wouldn't try to ruin your career just because I was jealous."

She sucked in an icy breath, stunned that he'd even consider such an idea. She hadn't meant to sound bigger by speaking up for all the members of her sex who'd been denied an equal opportunity, due not to any lack of talent or desire, but because of gender.

Jonnie remained silent as the waiter returned. He proceeded to take an incredibly long time on the ritual of wine delivery. When Dan had pronounced the golden Chablis acceptable and their glasses had been filled, Jonnie was finally given her chance to amend the misunderstanding.

"Are you going to propose a toast?" She smiled, lifting her glass.

He shrugged, looking disinclined to offer Jonnie Ryan anything at this moment but the door. "You're the women's libber, Jonnie. Why don't you?"

"You know where that is, don't you?"

"What?"

She still didn't have his interest, she could tell, as his eyes seemed to be focused somewhere past her left shoulder.

"A woman's libber," she explained quietly. "I asked you if you knew where it was."

He mumbled an inarticulate sound she took for a negative.

"Next to her kidneys." She grinned, the perky smile lighting up her face as she raised her glass. "To old friends," she suggested softly.

His lips twitched slightly as he seemed willing to give in. He raised his own glass, the fine crystal ringing out like a bell as it touched hers. "To old friends," he agreed. "And new beginnings."

Jonnie nodded, taking a sip. Then she reached out to cover his hand on the crisp white tablecloth.

"Please don't think I'm bitter," she said, her voice strained as she tried to make him understand she'd meant nothing personal by her remarks. "I never wanted to coach. I'm one of those people who believe that if God had intended us to fly, he wouldn't have invented flight insurance. I couldn't bear to spend all that time on those chartered planes, bouncing around the country."

She shivered slightly, her very real fear of flying sending an icy chill down her spine. Her first memory of flying was as a toddler when she survived the crash that took her mother's life. Jonnie closed her eyes for a moment, gathering strength to exorcise those horrors she'd never quite succeeded in putting behind her. The slight, reassuring squeeze of Dan's fingers, brought her mind back to the subject at hand.

She offered him a wobbly smile. "Besides, you know what they say about college coaching. Hang in there long enough, grit your teeth enough, and your orthodontist bills are bound to go up. I've no intention of wearing braces again at my age."

Dan relented, his harsh look softening as he turned her hand over, lacing his fingers through hers. "Your father had some big dreams for you."

"Dad's a big dreamer." Jonnie laughed lightly. "You'd think he'd be satisfied with one son being a high-school coach, another who's an assistant at UCLA and two other sons playing in the pros, wouldn't you? Without slapping a number on the back of his little girl's tank top and sending her out to play with the boys."

Dan eyed her over the rim of his wineglass. "As I recall, you could hold your own, Ryan."

Jonnie smiled at the memory, her expression warmly reminiscent. Recalling those days, she didn't notice the tender look in his eyes, riveted upon her.

"We used to pick up extra movie money that way." She shook her head at the antics she and her brothers had pulled in their younger days.

Dan blinked as her cloud of auburn hair settled back down over her shoulders. The candle flickering in the crystal glass between them sparked streaks of golden flame in her hair. He tightened his fingers around the stem of his wineglass to keep from reaching out to touch the fiery waves, to see if they were as warm as they appeared.

"Dan?"

At Jonnie's soft query he took his eyes from her brilliant hair, following her gaze to their entwined hands. His fingers were pressing into hers with an un-holy strength and he forced them open, freeing her hand. He watched the confusion coalesce in her eyes as she rubbed her fingers gingerly, bringing the blood back to the surface.

"I'm sorry," he answered, his voice unnaturally rough. "What were you saying about movie money?"

Jonnie had lost interest in the story herself as their eyes held, each one tentatively seeking some hidden message in the other's gaze.

"Nothing important. We'd just go to some neighborhood where no one knew us and make some side bets. Since none of the boys ever expected a girl to be able to play, we'd usually pick up enough to go to the movies."

Dan's ardent gaze held the impact of a physical caress as it broke free of her vaguely troubled eyes and moved across her face, drinking in her features as if he found her far more appealing than anything offered on the tasseled menu.

"I can imagine," he replied.

Although they were still managing to carry on a light conversation, there was an exchange far more stimulating occurring at the moment.

Jonnie didn't know how she managed it, but she answered with a shaky laugh. "The only problem was that once in a while I'd try it by myself, and nobody would pay up to a mere girl. Especially one who'd just humiliated a local in front of his peers. Jason would have to go collect for me."

"I can see where that would be an incentive to pay up," Dan agreed, granting the fact that her older brother's intimidating six-foot-eight-inch presence might prove sufficient motivation for anyone to consent to anything.

His darkening eyes settled on her lips, and Jonnie discovered, to her dismay, that she could no longer think of anything except what was happening here. It was as if they had been swept away into some sensual vacuum; all the murmuring of dinner conversation, the clattering of silverware and the occasional kitchen sounds receded into a far distant place. As if of its own volition, her body leaned toward him, and a spark of desire flared in his glittering blue eyes. Dan's hand lifted, as if guided by an inner force and moved to her lips, which parted slightly in anticipation.

Jonnie was torn between relief and regret when the waiter reappeared with their dinner order, shattering the provocative trance.

Dan remained silent, as shaken as she. Then, searching out safer ground, he cast a disapproving look at her plate.

"That's a terrible thing to do to Swiss cheese," he decreed. "What ever happened to piling it onto a ham sandwich smothered with mustard?"

"This happens to be a superb zucchini quiche," Jonnie retorted, relieved to be at odds with him again. This was much, much safer. "And besides—" she pointed her fork at his enormous plank of prime rib "—I never bite into anything that might bite back."

"Oh, Lord," he groaned, shaking his head. "Don't tell me you're a vegetarian as well?"

"As well?" A brow arched inquisitively, her green eyes handing him ample warning.

"As well as an attorney," he said, as if reminding her of something she'd forgotten. "I mean, one is bad enough. Especially when you make a living basking in the reflected glow of the political limelight. But Tom must've had holy fits when you started in on bean sprouts and lentils. I mean, that's a man who's firmly convinced they served a barbecue at the Last Supper."

Despite her rush of annoyance at the way he'd demeaned her chosen profession, Jonnie, knowing her father's penchant for burning thick slabs of beef to a charcoal crisp, had to smile at Dan's accurate description.

"It took him a while to realize I wasn't simply rebelling," she admitted. "On all counts. I'm the family pragmatist. I went to college for my law degree, not as a stepping-stone to an athletic career. I love my work. And I'm damn proud of it." The warning in her eyes hardened to agate. Again, he chose to ignore it.

"You're dead wrong on this one, Jonnie."

"How do you know that? You don't even know what I'm doing," she protested. "You just assume I'm out to get all the coaches in Oregon. Starting with you."

"Aren't you?"

"No!" The fervent exclamation came out louder than she'd planned. Well versed in discreet political behavior, Jonnie immediately lowered her voice, glancing around to see if she'd been overheard.

"I'm not at all," she objected. "I happen to be a member of a very respectable commission trying to ensure college athletes are treated fairly and honorably—by the rules."

"What if they're not always the same thing? Fairness and rules," Dan probed, his eyes narrowing as he speared her with an equally angry gaze.

"Rules are rules," Jonnie countered firmly. "They're created for a purpose—for order. It's up to all of us to see they're followed for the good of society."

"To the letter." His tone was grim.

"Precisely."

Dan pushed his plate away, suddenly losing all taste for the expertly prepared food. "I may have been wrong in the training room. You sure as hell don't sound like Tom Ryan's daughter right now, lady."

"That's because I happen to be Jonnie Ryan, an individual, and not some female clone of a man you once admired."

"And still do," Dan corrected swiftly. "As I recall, you once admired him."

That was out of line. Just because Dan was displeased with what she was doing, he had no right accusing her of not respecting her father.

"I still do! And it's those morals he taught me that make me so furious when I read about the too-soon-forgotten casualties of our collegiate sports system. Kids are being used until their eligibility runs out, then tossed aside like yesterday's newspaper, without a pro contract, an education or any means to earn a decent living. That's what the commission's all about, Dan."

"Bull." He shook his dark head, the expletive sharp and derisive. "That commission of yours is nothing but a well-orchestrated plan to get William Murdock elected attorney general. He's got you doing his dirty work, digging into whatever garbage you can uncover, in order to gain him some spectacular headlines."

Those same eyes that had been caressing her face with such warmth were now looking at her as if she'd just crawled out from under a rock.

"Talk about using the athletes, Jonnie. You're willing to win votes for the bastard at the expense of the school, the basketball program and the integrity and reputation of sports in general."

Jonnie's fork clattered to her plate. "That's not true. You make the commission sound like nothing but a cheap political stunt."

"That's all it is. I guarantee you won't be allowed to close up your little spy shop empty-handed, Jonnie. And if you aren't in on Murdock's reprehensible little trick, you're being used too, sweetheart. So welcome to the club."

Jonnie shook her head firmly, the russet color catching the brilliant light from the candle between them. But this time, Dan Kincade's mind was on something else altogether.

"I won't believe a word of what you're saying, Dan. I've worked with William and know him to be honestly concerned about the problem of collegiate athletics. I'll admit—" she dropped her tone a register, attempting to calm down before she succeeded in creating a scene "—his reputation in legal and political circles might be a bit tough. The man likes to win." She gave him a long, pointed look. "Just like the rest of us."

Jonnie observed the heavy sigh of frustration that lifted and dropped Dan's broad chest. "If you haven't done anything wrong, Dan, we have no problem," she pointed out.

He put his rumpled napkin on the table, shaking his dark head. "It must be nice to see things with such simple black-and-white clarity, Jonnie. In a weird sort of way, I find myself actually envying your neat, precise little world."

The silence eddied about them as they returned to the now-deserted athletic facility. Jonnie refused the loan of Dan's jacket this time, causing his eyes to flare with an irritated fire, but he didn't insist. Her high heels rang out in the empty hallway as her long strides easily kept up with him.

"Care to work off a little of that zucchini?" Dan stopped at the gym door.

"Work," Jonnie replied, continuing on toward his office, refusing to be sidetracked this time. A few more paces and she realized she'd lost him. Retracing her steps, she found him in the gym, a single dim bank of lights turned on, casting long, eerie shadows.

"Would you please come back to your office?"

"It's too late for work." Dan rejected her tautly issued demand. "But there's always time for a little one-on-one. Want to see if you still have the moves, Jonnie?"

She stared up at him, not knowing whether to scream, laugh, or cry. The man had quite effectively managed to keep her away from his precious records the entire day. Now he had the nerve to suggest she play basketball with him.

"Even if I wanted to, which I don't," she said firmly, "this isn't exactly a regulation uniform I'm wearing, Dan. In case you hadn't noticed."

Dan's eyes took a leisurely survey of her body, skimming the curves enhanced by the emerald silk shirtwaist dress.

"Oh, I've noticed." His roving gaze seemed to warm her as it continued its slow appraisal. "But if you unbutton your skirt a few more buttons from the bottom, it should give you enough freedom. And you can take off the heels and play in your stocking feet."

Dan grinned boyishly, coaxing her further. "I promise to go easy. I won't work you so hard you get sweaty, Ryan."

"You paint such an attractive picture," Jonnie shot back dryly. "I thought we'd at least managed to agree that I'm not that freckled-faced girl who reminded you of your kid sister."

Suddenly, the mood changed. Dan's gaze fixed on her face for an unbearably long time, his cobalt eyes seeming to consume her. Jonnie was powerless to move as he reached out a long finger, trailing it along her wide, generous mouth. The silent appraisal seemed to go on endlessly, a puzzled frown cutting little lines between his black eyebrows.

Jonnie couldn't have budged an inch if her life had depended on it. For a long, silvered moment, she was unable to drag her incredulous gaze from his lips. Then her gaze traveled upward, the shock jolting her to her toes as her soft green eyes suddenly clashed with the infinity of his blue ones.

The fingers that moved along her face with such tenderness followed her jawline, down to cup her chin, tilting her face. Jonnie watched the dark flare of raw male desire suddenly spark in the cobalt depths, as her own eyes gave him the answer to the yet unspoken request.

"You realize we've got ourselves a problem here, Ryan." Dan's voice was rough, the husky timbre uneven as he stared down at her softly bewildered expression.

"A problem?" she echoed, as if the words were unfamiliar to her.

"A potential powder keg," he affirmed soberly. "And if either one of us possessed one iota of sense we'd take off running right now."

"I've always had a theory about danger."

Despite his best intentions, Dan's long fingers curled about her waist, massaging lightly. "I'm not at all surprised." He laughed raggedly. "Since you seem to have an opinion about everything else."

"You never solve anything by running away, Dan. Tom Ryan taught me that lesson long ago, and I know darn well he taught you the same thing."

"I don't remember him advising me to go out of my way to find trouble, either."

She smiled, a gilt-edged invitation in her bold green eyes. "Fools rush in..." she murmured.

Instinct prompted Jonnie to close her eyes, but she fought against it, watching as Dan's dark head lowered, mesmerized by the kiss she knew was finally coming. That kiss she'd dreamed about over and over during her adolescence, but never tasted. Unconsciously, her tongue moved along her lips, moistening them, as if preparing for his touch.

The provocative gesture made Dan groan and Jonnie felt his sharp intake of breath as his lips touched the moist, parted curve of her mouth. A sense of delicious warmth came over her as she leaned into the kiss and her lids fluttered closed. Rising up on her toes, she delighted in the seductive magic of his lips as they touched hers with a silky caress. Her hands encircled his neck, playing with the soft curls brushing the top of his collar.

It was evidence of Dan Kincade's vast store of restraint that his kiss demanded nothing from her. At the same time, his lips were not at all tentative as they explored what Jonnie so willingly offered. His tantalizing tongue glided along her teeth, teasing with its tip, but never moving to enter the dark cavern of her mouth.

Then, a deep tremor, which shook his hard body, was echoed by the heated flash of pure need that suddenly forked through Jonnie like a jagged bolt of lightning. Her soft, breathless cry caused Dan to lift his head, pulling back slightly, twin fires blazing in his eyes.

"Dynamite," he murmured, not appearing at all happy about the desire she knew was echoed in her own eyes. "Pure TNT."

Momentarily abandoning her lips, Dan rained a blizzard of tiny, tingling kisses over Jonnie's uplifted face. His strong hands moved from her hips to her breasts and back again, stoking fires under the gleaming green silk.

Jonnie Ryan was not without experience, but the searing heat of pure physical desire forcing its way through her was a torment she had never known. With blinding instinct, she suddenly realized what it was to want a man. She wanted to hold Dan to her; she yearned to feel his life force surging deep within her yielding flesh, uniting them in the most erotic way possible. She caught his dark head in her palms and held him to a kiss that cried out the message of her fierce, desperate passion.

Dan growled deep in his throat, and his full lips became suddenly savage in their need as they molded her mouth with a force that took her breath away. Jonnie's head swam with a delicious vertigo, stars flashing on a background of ebony velvet behind her closed lids. Her fingers thrust through Dan's thick black hair, delighting in its silken texture.

She swayed under the drugging massage of his wide hands as they molded and lifted her hips, and when he spread his legs, urging her into hard, intimate contact, tiny shivers of anticipation coursed through her. Jonnie knew, as her body clamored for more of his expert touch, that this was no adolescent girl's dream. Her pliant body pressed against him, moving in sensual circles with all the provocative invitation of a woman.

The only sound in the cavernous gymnasium was their uneven breathing and the rustling of Jonnie's silk dress. The material offered scant barrier to Dan's palms as her nipples responded to his touch, hardening to taut little buds. Their sensual response acted as a further aphrodisiac to desires that were already running rampant through Dan's loins. He suddenly realized that if he kept drinking from her gloriously sweet mouth and Jonnie kept moving against him in this painfully inviting manner, he'd be tempted to take her right here on the gymnasium floor, under that new electronic marvel of a scoreboard.

The tawdriness of that idea, combined with the tender feelings he'd once held for her as a girl, conspired to side with common sense. He slowly brought his hands to Jonnie's shoulders, sighing heavily as he moved her away from him.

A short, potent silence swirled around Dan and Jonnie as they observed each other gravely, two pairs of eyes still sharing the darkened shadows of unfulfilled desire. Something had just inexorably altered their relationship, and it was obvious neither one was quite certain how to handle the change.

"That wasn't," Jonnie said finally on a breathless, shaky little laugh, "exactly a brotherly kiss."

There was another little pool of silence as Dan appeared even more confused than she. His blue eyes took on a strange expression as they moved restlessly across her flushed face.

"No, it wasn't, was it?" A vague note of contrition roughened his deep voice.

"Hey," Jonnie objected with a crooked smile, "if you dare apologize, I'm going to be furious. I enjoyed it, Dan. Quite a bit, actually."

"So did I."

For a man who'd allegedly just shared a terrific kiss, Dan sounded more like he was on the way to the gallows. Jonnie suddenly realized that while she'd always thought of Dan Kincade as a man, he'd last known her as a child. No wonder he seemed to feel guilty. The eight-year difference in their ages, while of no consequence now, had been an immeasurable gulf back then.

Although Dan's eyes could acknowledge the obvious fact that Jonnie Ryan was now a mature young woman, his mind still hadn't completely accepted that fact. He was still staring at her in a bemused fashion, and she touched his arm lightly.

"I should be getting home."

Dan gave a short shake of his head, as if to dispel the lingering attraction. "Of course. Where are you staying?"

"Home," she repeated, deciding to elaborate when she saw his still-confused expression. "You know, one of those little white frame things with a wide porch in the front and a couple of rose bushes and a Chinese elm tree in the backyard. It's old and it's small. But it's mine."

Jonnie watched his brow furrow in disbelief. "You're planning to commute every day?"

"It's only sixty-two miles," she reminded him. "And it's all Interstate."

Dan frowned. "It's too late for you to be driving back to Salem tonight. Boy, Jonnie, for a supposedly intelligent female, you sure seem to be making some dumb decisions lately."

Jonnie was suddenly bone weary. She was depressed by the fact she had done no work today. Her nerves were on edge from the emotional buffeting they'd received from this reunion. One thing she didn't need was Dan Kincade's high-and-mighty tone of male superiority.

"I hadn't realized we'd still be wandering along these hallowed hallways well after the janitors had gone home," she snapped, fatigue making her irritable.

"I don't keep bankers' hours, Ryan. You, of all people, should know coaching is damn hard work."

She glared up at him. "I'm not opposed to hard work, Dan. Believe it or not, I've some acquaintance with it myself. But this hasn't been work. It's been one continual cat-and-mouse game since I showed up here. I've wasted an entire day because you had to show me just who was in charge. Home-court advantage, right?"

Dan rubbed the back of his neck, his wide shoulders slumping beneath the tweed jacket. He was as tired as Jonnie looked, and he felt a vague stab of regret for what he'd done, even if it'd seemed appropriate at the time.

"You probably have something there," he grudgingly admitted. "And when you put it that way, it makes me sound like a real bastard."

Jonnie stood her ground as he looked down at her with a look that invited her comment. She'd be damned if she was going to deny that statement.

He raised his hand in the gesture of a pledge. "I promise you can see whatever you want tomorrow. Whenever you want."

Jonnie eyed him warily, her sharp eyes seeking the trap. This was too abrupt a change of face for her orderly, legal-trained mind to easily accept.

"Honest?"

"Scout's honor." Dan nodded in confirmation of his words. "You just name a time and I'll have everything ready."

"Nine o'clock," Jonnie said, wanting to get it over with as early in the day as possible. *To avoid the long drive back home at night, she told herself. To avoid the intimacy of having dinner with him again,* an unruly little voice in the far reaches of her mind piped up.

"Within reason," Dan argued. "You can't get down here that early and still get enough sleep tonight. Make it later."

Jonnie ground her professionally straightened teeth, making mental apologies to her father and her orthodontist for the damage she'd inflicted on them since arriving on campus this afternoon.

"Dan, would you try doing me a favor?"

"What kind of favor?"

He wasn't going to be a pushover, that was for sure. She wondered how many other people would automatically answer that question with an immediate agreement. But not Dan Kincade. Didn't the man trust anyone?

"Would you forget you ever knew a scarecrow of a kid with a mop of wild red hair? I don't need another big brother, Dan. Why don't you try pretending I'm just any other woman."

She'd walked right into it, eyes wide open. Jonnie Ryan, Law Review, top of her graduating class at Willamette University, had just been dumb enough to give the man an opening a mile wide.

"I believe that was precisely what I was doing when things began to get out of hand," he stated, grinning with devilish insinuation.

"Whoa," she corrected. "Let's try that again. How about treating me like any other attorney, here to check out your program?"

He ruffled her hair with easy familiarity. "Make up your mind, Jonnie. Do you want me to pat that nice firm little rear or put a boot to it?"

"A compromise position would be nice," she invited with a light laugh.

Dan joined her in the easy laughter, his hand lightly on her back. As they reached the parking lot, he shrugged out of his jacket once again, placing it over her shoulders.

"Really, Dan. This isn't necessary."

"Humor me," he insisted softly, not for the first time. Good Lord, Jonnie thought, wasn't that precisely what she'd been doing all day long?

"Is that bilateral?"

"Are you asking if I'll humor *you* tomorrow?"

"I mean," she clarified, "will you agree not to make any judgments about my work until you see me in action?"

Jonnie felt a warmth flowing through her, which had nothing to do with the heavy jacket, as Dan reached out and rubbed at the furrows on her forehead, erasing them under his sensuous fingertips.

"I'll do my best, Ryan. But you're asking a lot. I think we were better off when you just wanted me to think of you as a woman."

Jonnie stared into the clear-blue depths of his eyes for what seemed an eternity. A shiver danced along her spine as she read a message that was anything but fraternal.

"We'd better get you on your way," Dan said, his eyes suddenly unreadable. "And Jonnie—"

"Yes?"

"Any time you show up tomorrow is fine. I'll fit my schedule to your timetable." A corner of his mouth twitched slightly, and Jonnie knew he was referring to her earlier outburst.

"Thank you," she murmured, pulling her keys out of her purse and unlocking the door of her car. When she started to take off the jacket, Dan caught her by the lapels, urging her to keep it.

"Bring it back tomorrow." The rain had stopped but the night air was heavy with moisture. She could see it glistening like diamonds in his black curls.

"You'll get cold," she argued.

"No, I won't. I'll think about you." His deep baritone voice held a husky intimacy that certainly succeeded in warming Jonnie.

"Now I'm an alternative energy source." She laughed, backing away from the renewal of that bittersweet desire that seemed to spark so easily between them.

Dan didn't share in the laughter this time, his hands remaining on the edges of the lapels. "I really don't like you driving alone at night like this."

"I'll be fine."

"Will you call me when you get home?"

Jonnie's eyes widened. She'd been brought up to be independent. Tom Ryan had never waited up for her on a single date, treating her in the same manner he had Jonnie's four older brothers. He'd trusted her and known his only daughter to be sensible enough to stay out of situations which might prove dangerous. Now here she was, at twenty-eight, being asked to check in after a simple hour's drive on what was probably, by now, a deserted freeway.

"That's silly," she protested.

"Jonnie—"

She sighed resignedly. "I know. Humor you, right?"

That brought a slow smile to his face. "You've got it," he answered. "I won't sleep a wink if I'm worrying about you. And you've no idea how uncooperative I can be when I'm tired."

"I thought that was when you were hungry."

Something sparked between them, sending Jonnie a thousand messages—each and every one of them extremely provocative.

"That, too. Men do have certain basic needs, Jonnie."

As tired as she was, Jonnie still maintained enough sense to keep her from picking up on it.

"I'll call you," she agreed, opening the car door.

"Jonnie?"

She turned as she slid into the bucket seat, having to look a long way up at him. "Yes, Dan?"

"Why don't you arrange to stay in town while you're working here at Cascades? That's too much of a drive to do twice a day. Especially with all this rain."

"It always rains in the Willamette Valley, Dan. That's why everything is so nice and green. I'm well acquainted with slippery roads."

The look he gave her was half-angry, half-amused. "Are you always this damn stubborn?"

Jonnie smiled sweetly. "So I've been told."

Dan bent, leaning his head into the open door, brushing her lips lightly, tenderly. Then he rubbed his knuckles lightly against her cheek.

"Think about it, okay? I'd feel a lot better. And I'm not asking of you nearly what you're demanding of me."

Jonnie jerked her head back, breaking the velvety contact. "Now what are you talking about?"

"All I'm asking you to do is make one little change in your living arrangements for a few days. You're insisting I open up my life and the lives of all my players to public scrutiny. I'd say you're bound to come out ahead in all this, Jonnie."

She looked straight out the windshield, refusing to meet what she knew would be a chastening look.

"I'll think about it," she muttered, turning the key in the ignition to bring the car to life.

"That's my girl," he murmured, more to himself than to her as he shut her door.

The sporadic sprinkling of rain had begun again, and Jonnie watched as Dan hunched his shoulders against the cold drizzle, his hands thrust deep in his pockets as he turned to walk back toward the darkened athletic complex.

It could have been simply the weather that caused his downcast appearance, but Jonnie would've bet against it. No, she had the feeling this had something to do with her and her work on the commission.

When she'd accepted the appointment, Jonnie had been thrilled, knowing it was her unique athletic background and strong legal credentials that had earned her the post. She'd thrown herself into the work with all the zeal of a crusader seeking the Holy Grail. It had admittedly bothered her, in the back of her mind, that there could be some unpleasantries if she turned up illegal or unethical activities.

But never in a million years had she considered the consequences of finding Dan Kincade guilty of such transgressions. Now, risking a glance in her rearview mirror, Jonnie realized the day might come when she'd have to face that possibility. Something was bothering the hell out of the man—and she knew it wasn't the fact that he missed her freckles.

Chapter Three

Jonnie did as promised; calling Dan as soon as she walked in the door. She told herself it was only to keep him from worrying. It had nothing to do with her desire to hear that deep voice once more.

"Thank God you made it home safely. Now I can breathe again."

His voice rolled over her like a soft cashmere blanket, banishing any chills remaining from the damp night air. Jonnie hugged Dan's jacket about her, inhaling the enticing mixture of scents trapped in the gray wool tweed. A woodsy after-shave, mingled with the pungent aroma peculiar to damp wool, a faint hint of smoke from the candle that had glowed between them at dinner, and a unique masculine scent that would have enabled her to recognize Dan Kincade if she'd been blind.

"Your concern is appreciated, Dan, but totally unnecessary."

"I can't help how I feel," he objected, his voice a low grumble. "Although it could be argued I haven't displayed a wealth of consistency toward you today, you do manage to bring out a protective streak in me a mile wide, Ryan."

"That's very reassuring, Kincade," Jonnie answered flippantly, "but just who's going to protect me from you?"

She could hear the roar of laughter as if he were standing right there beside her. "When it comes to keeping away unwanted admirers, Jonnie, you've got a regular battalion. Four older brothers and your father, every one of them bigger than me."

She joined in the laughter, thinking as she did so that she didn't really want to be protected. Not from Dan. Then, as he changed the subject, she assured him she'd give thoughtful consideration to his request about taking a hotel room in Eugene while she was working at the college. There was a brief, significant silence. Then, with nothing left to say, Jonnie murmured good night and hung up, staring at the telephone for a long time.

Exhausted as she was, Jonnie's mind refused to permit sleep, turning over the events of the day, analyzing them, seeking rational explanations for this tumultuous range of emotions. She had to admit that Dan Kincade's magnetism was every bit as strong as it had been all those years ago. Stronger. Because now

Jonnie was a woman and knew what she wanted. *It's only physical*, she assured herself. *Only chemistry.*

Jonnie's well-ordered mind preferred to go straight to the point; this confusion was an unwelcome, alien feeling. An intrusive thought hinted that her interest in Dan Kincade was more than simple sexual attraction. Could it possibly be an unexpected rekindling of her young, innocent love? Or was the man simply a challenge?

It was a harsh question, but Jonnie imposed her strict code of morality as harshly on herself as she ever used it on others. She detested lying and dodging issues and refused to permit it now. If it was only her need to prove once and for all that she could win Dan Kincade, then she was no better than that breed of predatory male who staked out women as conquests. She was no better than Michael Cunningham.

At the thought of the man she'd once seriously considered marrying, Jonnie pulled the blanket over her head, forcing her mind to concentrate instead on a misty-green vision of the rain forest growing along the coast. The musty scent and verdant growth finally lulled her to sleep, as it never failed to do.

Jonnie groped blindly for the switch on her clock radio. It couldn't be morning yet; she felt as if she'd just gotten to sleep. Forcing open one sleep-hazed eye, she looked over at the lighted green digital reading. With a deep groan she rolled over onto her back, staring bleakly up at the ceiling.

Whatever else Dan had been wrong about, the one thing he'd hit right on the button was the fact that commuting back and forth between Eugene and Salem would be more demanding than she could handle. She'd take his advice and move into a hotel for a few days. In fact, she'd throw a few things into a suitcase in just a few minutes. After she took her shower. In just one minute....

The insistent clamor of the phone jarred her awake, and Jonnie sat bolt upright, grabbing the receiver and grating out a harsh, disoriented, "Hello?"

"Damn. I woke you."

She slumped back onto the pillow, her glance sliding over to the clock. She'd gone back to sleep for more than three hours. Now that was demonstrating a fine degree of professionalism!

Jonnie struggled for dignity. "Of course not. I was just...uh...packing."

"You're going to stay in town." Dan's low voice had a pleased, satisfied ring.

"You're right about the drive. I've decided to stay down there the rest of the week and return home Friday."

"Do you think you'll have things all wrapped up by then?" His tone was casual, but Jonnie could sense how important her answer was to him.

"I don't know," she answered honestly, failing to give him the response she knew he wanted. "But the commission meets on Monday, so I'll be expected to give William some data before then."

"Right." Dan's tone was flat, and a lengthy silence followed the monosyllabic response. "Well, I just called to see what time you wanted to get together."

"I'll be down there in an hour and a half," she promised. "And Dan, don't worry. If you can't work with me, just sit me down in any old corner with a stack of files, and I'll be able to decipher them. I'll pack my Captain Midnight decoder ring," she added lightly.

"Yeah." His mind was obviously elsewhere. "See you later then."

"Later," Jonnie echoed, wishing he'd sounded more welcoming. She experienced a disquieting mental image of Dan, his blue eyes glued to the northern horizon, awaiting her arrival with all the impending dread of a farmer expecting a plague of locusts.

A different coed was seated behind the desk outside the closed office door this morning, and Jonnie mused about those obvious perks which came with being a winning coach at a college renowned for its winning tradition. She had not a moment's doubt that anything Dan Kincade wanted around here, he'd get. Including a ready supply of fresh-faced, cheerleader-pretty secretaries.

"I'm Jonnie Ryan," she introduced herself. "I'm here to see Dan Kincade."

The girl's smooth brow furrowed. "Oh. Well, Coach Kincade is in a meeting right now. With Mr.

Harrison, the athletic director. Would you care to come back later?"

Yesterday Dan's absence would have sent red flags waving. Today, however, Jonnie had a new handle on the problem. She smiled.

"That's all right. I don't need him to begin my work. If you could just bring me the transcripts of the team members, I can get started."

The horizontal lines on the flawless ivory skin deepened. "Gee, I'm afraid I can't do that. Those records are college property. Confidential college property," she added pointedly.

Jonnie fought down the quick flash of irritation. Obviously when Dan had left instructions that the commission's investigator was to be cooperated with, he'd neglected to leave her name. This lovely young thing was probably expecting a man. It was an understandable mixup.

"I understand," Jonnie replied smoothly. "But you see, I'm here from the Murdock Commission."

Baby-blue eyes regarded her blandly, not appearing at all moved by the revelation. Jonnie decided to try again.

"Coach Kincade assured me I'd be able to look at anything I wished today. I'd like to begin with the transcripts," she instructed briskly, her tone that of a woman used to getting her own way.

But her hard-earned air of authority failed to change the polite, blank stare.

"So—" Jonnie smiled encouragingly, reminding herself of that old axiom about flies and honey "—if you'll just get them for me, I'll be able to stop bothering you and let you get back to your studying." She nodded a russet head in the direction of the thick textbook the girl had been poring over.

Honey-hued locks skimmed the cashmere-clad shoulders as the blonde shook her head. "I'm sorry, but those records are college property; I'd need permission to give them to you."

Jonnie counted to ten slowly, allowing herself time to cool down. Even if Dan had erected yet another of his manipulative roadblocks, it was certainly no reason to take it out on his secretary.

"I've told you," she coaxed. "I've already received permission. Coach Kincade assured me last night I'd be free to see whatever I wished. And I'd like to begin with the transcripts."

The last was tacked on as a brisk order, and Jonnie had the urge to stamp her foot—an urge she managed to squelch, relying on the professional composure that had been so difficult to acquire. The genetic imprint of generations of hot-headed Irish ran deep in her veins, displayed vividly by her thick mane of fiery hair.

As if bored with the entire conversation, the girl shook her head more firmly. Glossy pink lips firmed as she demonstrated she was definitely not as malleable as the pastel colors of her skirt and sweater might indicate. She returned her attention to her studies, effectively cutting off further conversation with Jonnie by a thick curtain of blond hair.

"I'm sorry. I need permission and Coach Kincade didn't leave any instructions about you. If you'd like to come back after his meeting...." Her voice drifted off as she licked the tip of her finger and flipped a page, displaying an avid interest in the events preceding the Boer Wars.

"I'll wait," Jonnie snapped, sitting down in a chair just outside the office door.

"Fine." The golden head didn't lift from the textbook.

Jonnie waited, swinging her foot angrily as she crossed her legs, fuming with every Roman numeral the minute hand passed on her slim wristwatch. Had Dan been lying to her last night? He'd made no bones about his objections to this entire investigation, but he *had* promised to help. What in the world was he up to now? And more to the point—why?

Jonnie had just decided to storm the sacred sanctum of the athletic director's office, demanding cooperation from Dan, when she heard footsteps. Dan turned the corner, smiling in warm greeting as he spotted her.

"Coach Kincade—" the blond head snapped up as the girl effectively drew his attention from Jonnie "—this lady wants to see you."

"I know, Kimberly," he said with a nod. "Thanks." His smile widened to a devastating grin. "Jonnie, come on in. I'm sorry if you were kept waiting. But, when E.G. Harrison calls...." Wide shoulders lifted in a helpless shrug.

"I know," Jonnie replied dryly, entering his office suitably prepared by her long wait for the impending battle. "But what I don't understand, Dan, is why you left instructions that I wasn't to see anything again today. I thought we'd agreed to stop playing games."

Dan's eyes widened in what appeared to be honest surprise. "I don't understand. I told you, anything you want, you'll have."

"Unfortunately you forgot to tell Kimberly," she grated out, still irritated by the stubborn behavior of the attractive young receptionist.

"Kimberly! That's it." Dan's wide hand slapped his forehead and his expression became one of sudden comprehension.

Jonnie wished dearly she could share whatever was running through his devious mind. "I see. Kimberly is the secret word for today, right? And now the duck will come down and give me a hundred dollars."

His ruggedly handsome face took on a boyish appeal as he grinned, shaking his head. "No, but I'm afraid you're the first victim of finals week. Obviously Kimberly is filling in for Janet. Normally, Janet works mornings three days a week and afternoons two days. Kimberly, vice versa. But they must've switched after I left for the meeting. So—" he grinned triumphantly "—with Janet worried about exams, the message about you obviously slipped her mind. And Kimberly, despite that pretty marshmallow exterior, is hard as nails about rules. Just like some other lovely lady I know." The light danced in his crystal-blue eyes, encouraging absolution.

Jonnie had to admit the excuse sounded plausible. Heaven knows, she wanted to believe him. Because if Dan was attempting to head her off again, what could it mean except he had something to hide? And that was a thought too abominable to consider seriously.

"That's probably it," she agreed finally.

"Good. I'm glad we got that settled." He glanced up at the large institutional clock over the doorway. "How about some lunch before we get started?"

A prickly feeling skimmed up Jonnie's spine, raising the short hairs at the back of her neck. If *this* wasn't stalling, she'd just been elected Homecoming Queen.

She crossed her arms, eyeing him suspiciously. "Dan, you're giving me the distinct impression you don't want me to get any work done."

"I did wake you this morning, didn't I?"

"All right, so I went back to sleep," she admitted reluctantly, wondering what the question had to do with her allegation. "But it's not something I normally do. I'm usually irritatingly prompt." *Not like some people I know,* she could have added.

"I believe it," he agreed instantly, flashing Jonnie a brilliant smile that under normal conditions could set her heart fluttering. But not now. Not while this problem was buzzing about in her brain. "What I'm concerned about is the fact that you were probably in such a hurry to get down here you skipped break-fast."

"I didn't skip it." Jonnie relented under Dan's steady gaze. "I didn't skip it," she repeated firmly, "because I never eat breakfast."

"But you do eat lunch, don't you?"

"Yes, but—"

"Good. We'll just get a bite at a little place right off campus and be back here in no time at all."

Dan put his hand on her back, guiding her with gentle but persistent force out the door. He stopped at the desk where Kimberly was still bent over her book, as if attempting to absorb the knowledge in the thick text by osmosis.

"What do you need first?" Dan asked Jonnie in an accommodating manner.

"Transcripts."

"Kimberly, while we're at lunch, please pull the transcript records of all the players for Miss Ryan. We'll be back in an hour."

"An hour! But Dan—"

"An hour," he repeated to Kimberly, ignoring Jonnie's sputtered protest. As they left he said, "It's not good to bolt your food, Ryan. Do you have any idea how uncooperative I can be when I'm suffering from indigestion?"

Jonnie pressed her lips into a tight line as she looked up into his teasing blue eyes. "If what I've experienced so far is any indication of your compliance,

Coach Kincade, I shudder to imagine how you'd be if you were attempting to be difficult.''

Dan looped his long arm casually about her shoulders. "An hour it'll be," he reiterated, obviously quite pleased with his ability to control matters once again. "How about walking? It's a gorgeous day." He squinted up into the clear sky. "Would you look at that sun? I was beginning to forget how bright it could be."

Jonnie's worries vanished as she enjoyed her lunch. Dan appeared more like his life in the pros. There were tales of missed planes, nights spent on hotel-room floors because the beds were too short, and NBA owners who shuffled players around like a deck of playing cards, with the owners always looking for that elusive ace.

"Got so you'd need a program to know who was in the locker room with you," he alleged. "I knew one guy whose kid went to three kindergartens in three different cities. Imagine."

"Imagine," she echoed, wondering just how disruptive that could be for a child. A small frown etched its way into her forehead as she considered her older brother, Jason. His four-year-old daughter, Emily, couldn't wait to begin school. Then she remembered how close her brother's family was. Love, Jonnie decided, could overcome any obstacles.

"I never could understand guys who wanted to get married and play the game," Dan muttered, stirring a spoonful of sugar into the black coffee. "The two are definitely incompatible. You can't have a sports career and a family."

"I think you're wrong about that, Dan." Jonnie leaped to the defense of her brother and father. "From what I've seen, if a man's willing to make a strong commitment to his family, everyone can make the situation work. As for growing up in different cities, I did. And I never minded."

A black brow arched disbelievingly. "Never?"

"Well, perhaps once in a while," she admitted. "But that was probably due to my height as much as anything else. I always felt like Gulliver in the land of the Lilliputians."

"You never showed it. Not from where I sat," Dan assured her. His gaze swept over her. "Are you still uncomfortable?"

Jonnie smiled. "No, I love it. And you know, I think it's actually helped my career."

He appeared honestly interested. "Really? How?"

"Women attorneys aren't the novelty they once were. Walk into the offices of any major law firm in the nation, and what do you see? The entire place awash in a sea of gray serge. Men and women alike, we all wear our corporate uniforms. It stands to reason all those dull suits and faces would blend into a homogenized blur."

Dan nodded thoughtfully, studying her assertion.

"That's my advantage," Jonnie explained. "Seventy inches of female, even clad in a business suit, isn't easily dismissed. I literally stand head and shoulders above the rest. Then add this red hair—well, to be honest, I think I might've dyed it this color if I hadn't been born with it. The combination is a natural attention getter."

Usually Jonnie wore her heavy hair in a topknot, neat and tidy. But in the past two days, she'd allowed herself the admittedly feminine vanity of leaving it loose. She knew she'd done it to appear attractive to Dan, just as she'd taken to wearing the softer, more feminine items of her wardrobe. She refused to allow herself a moment's guilt over her behavior. It was only natural, wasn't it? To want to show Dan how nicely she'd grown up?

"I think," he said slowly, "that if you were ever to touch that gorgeous hair with any type of dye, I'd be forced to turn you over my knee and give you the back of me hand, Jonnie Ryan."

Dan's deep voice lowered into the feigned brogue Jonnie could remember him teasing her with while he'd practically lived at the Ryan home during his four undergraduate years. Although his house was already bursting at the seams, Tom Ryan never seemed to mind one more mouth in a family that seemed to go through as much food in a week as the annual consumption of the Third World.

Jonnie's hand flew to her throat and she fluttered her eyelashes in mock surprise as she easily fell back into light banter.

"Why, Coach Kincade, are you threatening me? Or is that a promise?"

Her soft purr was definitely provocative, and Jonnie found herself waiting for Dan's response with a sense of expectation.

"Tom never should've raised you as one of the boys," he muttered. His chair made a harsh, grating noise as Dan pushed it back, standing up from the table. He counted out some bills and placed them on the table, signaling an abrupt end to their conversation. "A mother would've taught you not to respond so damn readily to a man's less-than-honorable passes."

Jonnie sucked in a sharp breath at the harshness in his tone. She longed to tell Dan he had a lot of nerve. It was only *his* passes she responded to. It was only *him* she wanted. Only *him* she loved.

Her mind skidded to a halt. Loved? She risked a glance at his closed, shuttered face and sighed, deciding her feelings were too difficult to explain in this crowded, sunlit sandwich shop. Especially since she hadn't figured them out for herself yet.

There had been a discernible drop in temperature while they'd been eating, a haze of clouds moving to cover the sun. Jonnie buttoned her caramel-toned suede jacket, wondering if it was the dismal gray sky or Dan's sudden, equally chilly attitude that had dampened her mood.

Back in Dan's office, she took the chair he indicated behind his desk as he went to retrieve the folders from Janet. Seeing the pert brunette at her station outside the office door gave Jonnie's spirits a slight lift. Certainly Janet's presence gave credence to Dan's explanation about the mixup this morning. And for the time being, that nagging little black cloud of doubt hovering distressingly in her mind disappeared.

"I'm impressed," she said, reading through the papers.

Dan pulled up a chair next to her and was reading over her shoulder. Jonnie would die before she'd admit it, but he was proving a serious distraction as she breathed in the familiar woodsy scent of his aftershave. She had to steel herself to keep from jumping when he lifted a swathe of her hair, brushing it back over her shoulder as he leaned forward to read what had caused her comment.

"Impressed about what?" His breath was warm on her neck and Jonnie felt that strange stirring deep within her again.

"The grades the players are maintaining," she answered, forcing her attention to remain on the manila folder in her hand. "It's amazing."

"Not so damn amazing, counselor," he corrected swiftly. "We coaches aren't all the two-headed monsters your commission is implying we are. At the College of the Cascades every member of the team has graduated on time since I arrived three years ago. And I'm not taking full credit because a helluva lot graduated before my tenure. Ask your dad. We've recently voted that a player won't be able to play his first year if he isn't qualified academically. But he'll still have four years of eligibility after that. That gives him five years to get his degree."

"I know about that ruling," Jonnie pointed out. "But you have to admit, Dan, that the big money from television revenues has changed the sport a lot. Don't you find—off the record—that coaches believe winning is the main thing, whatever happens to the players?"

"We are under a lot of pressure," Dan admitted slowly, his long fingers rubbing at the cleft in his jaw. Jonnie tried not to notice how the slanting afternoon sunlight made the hairs on the back of his hand glisten like black gold.

"And I won't deny it, Jonnie," he continued. "Off or on the record. But it's high time others began accepting some of the responsibility, too. Too many athletes were never expected to learn to read and write. They've floated through the system because they were talented at sports. What about high schools that make a kid a hero while allowing him to graduate with a second-grade reading level? What about college administrations that set a lower average for playing eligibility than the grade-point average required to graduate? And don't forget the alumni who put the financial squeeze on the school, effectively blackmailing the grants program if the team doesn't come up with a winning season."

Dan's mouth thinned. "Hell, Jonnie, the dumb athlete isn't born—he's systematically created."

"That's exactly what I've been trying to say," Jonnie pointed out calmly, as Dan's heated statement wound down. "And that's what the Murdock Commission is all about."

He was unable to suppress a short, harsh laugh. "Honey, you are either incredibly naive, overly ambitious, or as treacherous as a black widow spider. I still haven't figured out which."

"That's unfair," she gasped.

"No, it isn't. Because what your little group of headline grabbers is going to do will be far more damaging than any social injustice in the sport you're liable to dig up."

Jonnie stiffened her back and squared her shoulders, not realizing the movement thrust her full breasts provocatively against the soft topaz wool of her dress. "I can read these transcripts myself, Dan. Surely you've better things to do?" Her brisk tone invited him to leave. She was only doing her job. A job she believed in. Why was he being so hostile? ·

"As a matter of fact, I do," he growled in a harsh voice, worlds different from the teasing brogue he'd treated her to in the sandwich shop. "I'll be back in a couple of hours."

"I'll be here," Jonnie mumbled, refusing to meet his gaze as she reached for a new folder.

Dan shook his head as he viewed her methodical study of the computer print-out sheets.

"Unfortunately, I've no doubt about that," he retorted, leaving her to her work.

Chapter Four

Jonnie braced her elbows on the desk, cupped her chin in her hands and gazed unseeingly out the windows. She was oblivious to the slanting silver rain as she concentrated instead on Dan Kincade. As she'd professed during dinner last night, she was the pragmatist in the family. Jonnie Ryan was known to be logical, sensible, and not at all given to romantic fantasies. She knew what she'd felt for Dan so long ago had been merely a childish crush. A fanciful girl's dream of Prince Charming.

Dan had been handsome, intelligent, talented and popular. Even the more experienced coeds had trailed after him like worshipful puppies. A young girl just beginning to experience the first stirrings of womanhood would have had little resistance to falling in love with the man.

Now, however, she was older, wiser, and had learned the folly of giving your heart. She was no longer vulnerable to Dan Kincade's admittedly seductive appeal. And yet, something was happening. From the first moment she'd walked into his office, Jonnie had been experiencing these oddly unnerving emotions. There had been too many times she'd responded far more like a woman than a cool-headed attorney.

She had taken criticism about her work before; it came with the territory. She'd heard attorneys arguing the other side in the courtroom practically brand her a liar. She'd seen political cartoons portraying her as a power-hungry female dragon. And she'd read gossip columns that attempted to brand her a few things even more unattractive. But nothing had ever wounded her so deeply as Dan had these past few days with a muttered complaint or a sadly censorious look from those soulful blue eyes. The reason he was able to hurt her was that she cared so very, very much for him.

A copper coin suddenly clanked in front of her, twirling crazily on its edge. The spinning penny brought her mind abruptly back from her deep concentration.

She glanced up at Dan. "If that's for my thoughts, you're not very flattering. They should be good for a dime, considering inflation. A nickel, at the very least."

"Ah, but any more than this and I might be accused of bribing a state investigator," he retorted. "I didn't figure you'd send me to the electric chair for a simple penny offense. That *is* still a petty crime, isn't it, counselor?"

Jonnie's clear green eyes shadowed with distress. "Dan, surely after all the years we've known each other you don't believe I'm that win-at-all-costs woman you keep hinting about."

Dan Kincade perched on the corner of the desk and tunneled his hand under her thick hair. His long fingers massaged the back of her neck.

"That's part of my problem," he admitted on a deeply unhappy note. "I don't know you at all, Jonnie. You're different from that kid with the smart-alecky mouth filled with braces. You're worlds different from the worshipful little girl who gave me the privilege of being her first big crush...."

He sighed, his eyes moving over her face in a gentle manner. "To tell you the truth, babe, right now you scare the living daylights out of me."

His fingers continued their beguiling massage as he caught and held her gaze. Jonnie could feel the warmth induced by his caressing fingertips and knew her face was coloring with a rosy glow. If he only realized how much she still resembled that idealistic girl.

Oh, she no longer worshipped Dan Kincade. And she certainly no longer believed him to be perfection personified. But those early primitive feelings that had begun to stir in her so many years ago were threatening to blaze out of control with his every touch.

"I suppose this is a good a time as any to tell you I appreciate the way you treated me that day," Jonnie said softly. Her own hand left her chin and moved to rest on his thigh, which was only a few inches away on the scratched oak surface.

Dan's expression grew softer with the shared memory. "I'd seen it coming," he admitted. "And as much as I loved you, Jonnie, I think I was as terrified as you were that day. I was so damn afraid of handling it all wrong and damaging your future love life."

Dan's smile was slightly crooked as he covered her hand with his own, entwining their fingers. His thumb rubbed lightly against her palm. For a long, desperate moment Jonnie thought her heart would surely cease beating.

"You loved me?" It was a whisper.

Dan's fingers increased their pressure. "Of course I did, Ryan. Like you were my very own kid sister. In fact, I was going to talk to Tom about it, but you jumped the gun before I had a chance to obtain a little fatherly advice."

"Let's just drop the subject, okay?" Jonnie snapped, embarrassed that she'd allowed herself to misread his words. She turned her head, displaying an avid interest in the rainstorm outside.

"What the hell's the matter now?" Dan's hand moved from the back of her neck, grasping her chin as he jerked her gaze back from the rain-lashed window.

"Do you know," he grated with barely controlled frustration, "that you're about as capricious as this damn weather? I can't get a fixed signal on you at all."

"Me? Don't dump that on me! You haven't exactly been a model of constancy yourself, Daniel Kincade. I can't figure out whether you want me off this campus or in your bed."

"Both."

The single muttered answer stopped Jonnie's rising outrage in midthought just as she'd been gathering additional verbal ammunition. Her eyes widened as she watched Dan's hand move over his face, rubbing in a weary, defeated gesture.

"Come for a ride with me. We've got some talking to do."

"I've still got some transcripts...."

"Would you just forget the goddamn transcripts?" he roared. "You're driving me crazy in more ways than one, Jonnie Ryan. And if for no other reason than old-times' sake, you owe me the opportunity to get all this sorted out."

Is this where she was to learn what he was hiding, Jonnie wondered. Or was she being overly sensitive to every little nuance? Basketball coaches were well-known for their intensity. Perhaps she'd only been picking up on his internal pressures and misreading them. Getting everything out in the open would probably do them both a world of good. She'd spent far too much time today thinking about Dan instead of her work. It was behavior that no one who knew Jonnie Ryan would have recognized. She'd always been known for her Spartan work habits.

"Get what sorted out?" She realized Dan was still awaiting her answer.

"Us." He wasn't mincing words and his attitude was anything but inviting.

"It's a bad day for a drive." She wondered how they'd get anything accomplished with Dan attempting to keep his attention on the rain-slicked Eugene streets.

"We're not going far."

"Oh?"

"My place."

"Oh."

Jonnie offered him the cover of her navy umbrella as they left the sports complex, but Dan refused, walking beside her out to his four-wheel-drive Blazer. He held the door open for her, a hand under her elbow giving her a boost up, which she didn't need but appreciated anyway. At this point, any little human touch from the man was an improvement over the air of stiff formality he'd pulled down over his rugged features.

She studied the strong profile as he drove. His jaw was firmly set as he seemed to be marshaling his thoughts. A thin white line circled his mouth; a muscle jumped along his cheekbone, and nothing about him suggested a single nerve in his body was capable of relaxation. This might have been one huge mistake, she considered, knowing she'd make the same decision again. She had to know where they stood.

Dan wasn't about to give her a clue to his intentions as he led her into his house, gesturing for her to sit down while he lit the fire he'd obviously prepared before leaving for work. His two-story brick house was nestled in a heavily wooded area above the city. The living room was huge, accommodating Dan's oversized furniture. Multilevel decks filled the immense space between floor and ceiling, and the fireplace was at least twenty-six feet high, Jonnie guessed, her eyes moving a very long way upward. Stained-glass windows cast a warm tint, which was echoed in the symphony of rich textures and warm colors.

The kindling caught, and a warm, crackling glow began to dispel the lingering damp chill in the air brought on by the rain.

"This is a beautiful home, Dan. Simply lovely."

Dan seemed pleased by her softly spoken words as he rocked back on his heels for a moment, his roving gaze circling the room.

"I'm glad you like it. I spent my life planning this home. It's the first I ever had and I wanted it right."

"The first?" she asked vaguely, wondering if she had misunderstood.

"You know, all those years on the road—hotel rooms, and airplanes. I just rented apartments," he explained casually. He rose, taking her suede jacket and hanging it next to his on the coatrack.

"What can I get you? Wine? Brandy? I mix a mean martini."

Jonnie shook her head. "Nothing, thanks."

"Sure?"

A soft smile crossed her lips. "I'm sure. I've got the feeling I'm going to need all my wits about me. You look like a man with a lot on his mind, Dan."

He grimaced as he joined her on the couch. Jonnie caught her breath as he turned toward her, stretching his arm along the top, his fingers rubbing absently at the woven, earth-tone material.

"You called that one right, Ryan. Where do you want to begin? Work? Or the personal stuff?"

What she wanted, Jonnie realized with a shock of feminine need, was to taste Dan's firm lips, softening them with her own to a shape more appealing, less forbidding. Then she wanted to slip her hands under his soft Shetland sweater and feel the steady beat of his heart under her palm. She wanted to trace her fingertips along his hard chest, experiencing the tactile delight of the crisp ebony curls she knew would await her. And then—oh, Lord. If she allowed her imagination to run rampant much longer, she'd never make it through this discussion.

"Work," she decided reluctantly. "Why are you so antagonistic toward me?" she asked, breaking away from the enticing, sensual thoughts that were turning her mind away from the subject.

"Work," Dan agreed, appearing as if neither subject was on his hit parade of popular topics. "For the record, I'm not antagonistic toward you. Although I'll admit to a genuine concern about your intentions.''

"And if I prove to you I'm not plotting to tear apart college sports?"

His eyes held hers with unwavering strength. "Do you think that's possible? I told you, Ryan, if you can't see what the Murdock Commission is all about, then you're too naive to succeed even with the best of intentions."

"I'm not naive, Dan. Just concerned. There's a social injustice in collegiate athletics today that has to be resolved. Only two percent of college athletes ever sign professional contracts in football, basketball or baseball. Do you know what happens to the rest of them? Do you care?"

Dan sighed a deep, weary breath. "I care, Jonnie. Believe me, I care. But I've a gut feeling you're about to tell me what happens to the ones who don't make it."

"They end up young men out on the street without any marketable skills."

"Not all," he argued.

"Well, of course not all of them," Jonnie agreed, feeling Dan was purposely avoiding any attempt to consider her point valid.

"Remind me to introduce you to our point guard, Brian Bishop. He's an academic all-American team member, maintaining a perfect four-point average while playing basketball. He graduates this June."

"That's a very impressive fact, Dan, but he's still just one—"

Dan interrupted, his voice a bit roughened, and out of the corner of her eye Jonnie watched his fingers dig a little more harshly into the cloth of the couch.

"What's the matter, Jonnie? Is it too difficult to consider these statistics one at a time? So you can see the guy behind the number? He's the hardest worker I've ever known. Despite the fact he's a good head shorter than most anyone he's up against, Bishop is one of the most solid performers on the team. In addition to those grades and the team, the kid's married. He works during the summer at a lumber mill to supplement the scholarship money."

"Does his wife work, too?" Jonnie asked, curious about the logistics of such a marriage. The scholarship paid for tuition and books, but everyone knew the funds fell far short of an amount that allowed survival at today's prices.

"She used to. There were, uh, complications."

Jonnie wondered what caused the shattering of Dan's handsome face to an inscrutable mask as he fell silent. She'd been in law long enough to recognize a suddenly uncooperative witness. She waited, not wanting to press him.

After an immeasurable time, relief came in the form of a log collapsing, sending a brilliant flare of orange sparks into the air. Dan left her to take the brass-handled poker and rearrange the burning wood. Then he returned, practically throwing his lofty frame down beside her once again.

"You know, don't you, that I want to make love to you?"

His blunt assertion shocked her. Yes, she knew that. But she certainly hadn't expected him to admit it in such a grim, funereal tone.

"I thought you did," she murmured. "And surely you realize the feeling is reciprocated—even if the timing isn't right."

"I do." Dan bit the words off, as if they were bitter and unpleasant. "But it just isn't that simple, Jonnie. Not if you're who I think you are. And that's what I can't figure out."

"I don't understand."

"Are you on, uh, friendly terms with Murdock?" His dark gaze speared her, as if seeking to probe the answer from her soul and not merely her lips.

"Friendly?" she faltered. "Well, I suppose. I mean, we've worked together before. He's certainly helped my career."

"That's not what I mean."

Comprehension dawned and Jonnie wondered why she'd missed the veiled suggestion in the first place. More than one opposing newspaper had hinted she'd received the position on the commission because she was young and attractive. William Murdock had a reputation for appreciating attractive, intelligent women with the same gusto he found in vintage wines and fast cars.

"If you mean, am I sleeping with him," she snapped, her eyes shooting angry sparks, "the answer is no. I've always had a cardinal rule, Dan. I don't play where I work. Which means, I suppose, that it's time for you to take me back to the office. Right now."

That was it. She'd been doing her best, maintaining her temper under conditions that would have caused her to erupt far earlier had she not been trying so damn hard to prove to Dan she was a mature, capable adult. But he had pushed too far. She was on her feet, glaring down at him as she waited for him to make a move. Instead, Dan just exhaled a weary sigh and combed his fingers through his black curls.

"There's no need for the outraged female routine, Ryan. Please sit down."

Jonnie shook her head, staring at him as if seeing him for the very first time. "You're really something, do you know that? You've been nothing but trouble for me since I walked onto your damn campus yesterday. You kept me waiting, you used every stalling tactic in the book, and a few new ones you made up. You caused me to lose so much sleep last night I overslept, something I never do—"

"Really?" Dan's dispassionate expression became one of intense interest.

Jonnie tapped her toe impatiently at the interruption. "Really, what?"

"Did you really think about me last night? Did I really keep you awake?"

"Of course, dammit!"

"Please sit down, Jonnie."

He patted the soft cushion, inviting her to rejoin him. Unable to resist the appeal in those warm blue eyes, Jonnie acquiesced. It was only a compliance of sorts as she slouched down onto the couch, sulkily refusing to meet his enticing gaze.

"I thought about you, too."

He played with a long thick strand of her rich auburn hair, coiling it around his hand, weaving it between his long fingers as he spoke to her softly. The velvet words seemed a haunting caress, soothing away her irritation.

"I thought about this gorgeous vibrant hair spread across my pillow in tongues of flame," he murmured. His fingers slowly trailed across the planes and curves of her face, as if attempting to memorize every feature for later review. He traced a heated path along her cheekbones, down the slight tilt of her nose, across her lids, in the slight crevice below her lips.

"I thought about kissing this lovely face." Dan's fingers closed about the lobe of her ear, and he tugged slightly, releasing the pearl clip earring and dropping it into her lap. "I thought about taking little bites of this soft, pink ear." He traced the convolutions of the shell-like interior, then, with his fingertip, rubbed a provocative little circle at the pulse spot just behind her ear where Jonnie had dabbed some Calandre perfume that morning. The warmth of his touch seemed to be releasing the fresh green and woody tones anew, the essence swirling about them in a fragrant cloud.

Dan had done none of the things he'd described, but his enticing words seduced her with every bit of sorcery the actual events could have evoked.

"Is that all you thought about?" Jonnie's green eyes held golden lights as she shared in the sensual fantasy.

"No. Do you want to hear more?" The look he bestowed on her spoke volumes more than the simple inquiry. Jonnie leaned forward, encouraging the intimacy of continued touch.

"Yes. I want to know everything you were thinking about me," she whispered invitingly, her lips parting in unconscious welcome.

"I thought about rediscovering your freckles," he continued, his voice a deep rumble as his hands shaped her shoulders, moving down her arms. "And then I fantasized kissing them, one by one."

His heated gaze dropped to Jonnie's breasts as they rose and fell with each deep gulp of air she inhaled. She was growing more and more enraptured with his description of their imagined lovemaking.

"I thought about how your skin would taste, up every inch of these long, curvaceous legs, until I'd find you warm and welcoming. As if you'd waited all these years for me to come to you in just this way."

Jonnie could feel her body following the suggestion of his words, and knew she'd never wanted a man more in her life.

"And that's when it all hit me," Dan said flatly, turning away from the beautiful, erotic mood he'd spun around them. "If you were any other woman, I'd have experienced those satiny legs wrapped around me last night. Everything was pointing to us ending up that way."

"I asked you to think of me as any other woman," she reminded him softly.

"But you're not, Jonnie. You're Tom Ryan's daughter." Dan's voice held a flat, no-nonsense tone.

"He'd be pleased we care for each other, Dan." Jonnie carefully avoided the word love. "He loved you like one of the boys. You know that."

"I know. And I know he'd be more than happy to beat the hell out of me if I hurt his little girl. Which he wouldn't have to do. Because having to face myself in the mirror each morning would be punishment enough."

"I'm certainly not little, by the wildest stretch of imagination," Jonnie protested with a ragged laugh. "And you're not going to hurt me, Dan. I'm not a little girl; I'm a woman. And I know exactly what I'm doing."

"No, you don't." Dan's tone was hard and his blue eyes possessed a flinty, metallic hue. "Inside that lush, womanly body, you're still a wide-eyed adolescent, dreaming about romance and hearts and flowers. I'm talking about two people finding enjoyment in each other... for a time."

He emphasized firmly, "For a short time. When I was playing, I watched the married guys trying to juggle families and careers. It was always an impossible task—something had to give, and invariably the wives and kids ended up with the short end of the stick. I made the decision not even to consider marriage while I was in the pros. I'm not looking for any long-term commitments, Jonnie."

"May I at least point out you're not in the pros any longer?" she interjected dryly. "Besides, Dan, I have a career of my own to consider. I'm not looking for marriage, either."

He expelled a frustrated sigh. "I think you honestly believe that. But I've the distinct impression that while you may have left the braces behind, you've maintained that ability to become carried away by romantic idealism. You'd only end up getting hurt."

His face could have been carved from granite, Jonnie considered, watching his handsome features harden. Her hands twisted together in her lap as she considered his words. Was she capable of painting rosy pictures about something that was purely a shared physical attraction between a man and a woman? Had she read this situation wrong from the beginning because she'd wanted it to be so much more?

"I think you're wrong, Dan," she argued softly. "I'm not that silly adolescent girl any longer. I've taken care of myself; I'm doing well professionally. And I've managed to make it to the ripe old age of twenty-eight without having my heart broken. Although I'll admit to a slight wounding when I was thirteen, which was entirely my own fault." She smiled a weak encouraging little smile.

"You might be able to handle it, Jonnie, although I still think you're kidding yourself. But right now I don't know if I can handle it."

"I don't understand."

"Look, honey, don't forget that I watched you grow up for four very important, formative years of your life. I helped your Dad build that tree house in the backyard for you, and I was the one who took you to the emergency room when you broke your arm trying to play Tarzan after Greg took the ladder away."

Under ordinary circumstances, the memory of her brother's antics would have caused Jonnie to smile. But these were not ordinary circumstances. She remained silent, her heart aching as she viewed the anguish on his dark features.

"Hell, Jonnie, don't you see? There's a very large part of me that would feel like I was taking liberties with my kid sister!"

"Dan, that's...." Her words dropped off as she searched for an appropriate word.

"Ridiculous?" he grated out harshly. "Don't you think I know that? Up here?" He hit his index finger against his head. "But I can't help the way I feel, dammit. I know you, Jonnie Ryan. You're the kind of woman a man builds a house for. Has children with. The guy who marries you will plant a tree on the day each kid is born, and the two of you will spend your life watching them grow—the kids and the trees. Then you'll spend your golden years holding hands, walking along the river. Hell, there'll probably be a sunset in the background that'll make this thick, gorgeous hair look like molten copper.''

"And the entire scene will be orchestrated with violins and a harp now and then to add some class.... Aren't you laying it on a bit thick, Kincade?''

Dan grimaced, leaning his head back for a moment and shutting his eyes. His thick black lashes curled ridiculously on his cheeks and she smiled, in spite of her distress.

"With a trowel," he agreed, opening his eyes in time to catch the slight grin. "I'm glad to see you find this entire mess so damn funny.''

"That's not what I was smiling at, dummy."

"What was it then?"

"I was thinking how pretty your eyelashes were and how I know women who'd kill for them."

He shook his head. "That's a ridiculous thought to be having in the middle of a life decision, Ryan.''

"Can I help it if you're gorgeous, Kincade? You just make a woman forget all that important stuff like responsibility and good sense.''

He sighed heavily. Then, lifting her fingertips to his lips, he kissed each one lightly.

"Let's just take it a day at a time, Jonnie. Right now the situation is too loaded. Once you finish with your investigation, we can explore the personal side of

Jonnie Ryan and Dan Kincade. Who knows, I maybe wrong.''

''About what?'' Jonnie's heart fluttered a bit, but caution kept it from soaring with renewed hope. She was getting the distinct impression that nothing about this relationship was going to be easy.

''That you're still the hearts-and-flowers kid I remember. You may be able to prove to me you're the hardhearted career woman you claim you've grown up to be. The family pragmatist, right?''

''Right.''

Jonnie lowered her eyes so Dan couldn't see the pain he'd inadvertently caused her. Why couldn't he realize that it was possible to be a capable career woman and still have a heart that turned somersaults whenever she thought of him?

''Come on.'' He rose from the couch, taking her hand to lift her up.

''Where are we going?''

''I'm taking you back before I give in to my baser instincts.''

He planted a quick hard kiss on her lips before helping her into her suede jacket.

Skim over the investigation, Jonnie Ryan, she told herself as Dan drove her back to the college and her own car, *and you could finish the thing up in two or three days. In all probability Dan wouldn't cheat anyway, so what do you plan to find if you sift through everything with a fine-tooth comb?*

End the investigation and Dan will agree to a per-
sonal relationship. He'll make love to you in a way
that will surpass any other man you might ever meet.
Who knows, you might even convince him that he
loves you, too.

It was so simple. And so complicated. Because some
sixth sense was telling her that Dan Kincade had every
hope she'd take him up on the unusual proposition,
just to get her out of his records.

Chapter Five

During the week that followed, Jonnie tried to keep that errant suspicion at the far reaches of her mind. She tried to keep her thoughts on work, discovering that while the student athletes seemed willing to accept her presence, none of them were enthusiastic about having their private lives investigated. The Buckley Amendment, ensuring their right to privacy, required that before she could gain access to their grades, each student had to approve the release. This proved no problem, but they still eyed her as if she were a representative from the Spanish Inquisition force and they were suspected heretics.

One student, however, asked to tell his story. Jonnie agreed readily and invited Dan to hear her tape the interview.

"That's real friendly of you, Ryan," he kidded as they walked down the hall to the office he'd managed to commandeer for her stay at the college. "I figured you were going to hold all your cards close to your chest and make me read about your findings in the paper."

"It's just an interview, Dan. Not a legal summation...." She tensed somewhat as she considered the upcoming event. "As a matter of fact, I've no idea what Calvin Dunn is going to say. He just came to me last night before I left and asked to put his story on the record. I'd have been a fool to turn that down. Most of the kids seem to have developed lockjaw."

"You scare them, Jonnie. You should understand that. They're young, trying to do their damnedest to straddle both worlds—academic and athletic—and here you march in, all vim and vigor, wearing your cause like a chip on that lovely shoulder. What do you expect them to do—applaud?"

"I'm trying to help them."

"Perhaps they don't believe they need help," he pointed out quietly.

"Well, that may be the case," she admitted, thinking over the records she'd studied during the past days. "But, you can't deny there are hundreds out there who do. It's a national disgrace, Dan."

He stopped before the closed door of her temporary office, his hands resting lightly on her shoulders as he turned her toward him. His voice was laced with what appeared to be a soft warning.

"I know about the scandals, Ryan. I'm one of the jocks who can read, remember? But you're barking up the wrong tree here. Why don't you just admit it and pack up your briefcase and go back to Salem where you belong?''

''I'm not finished yet, Dan.'' Jonnie met his gaze evenly.

''Oh, you're finished, sweetheart. You just haven't realized it yet,'' he muttered. He dropped his hands from her shoulders and nodded toward the door. ''Well, madam spider, shall we enter your parlor? I believe the victim awaits.''

Calvin Dunn rose from his chair as they entered, all seven feet of him. He appeared unnerved at seeing Dan with Jonnie, and she wondered if she'd made a tactical error. In her attempt to bend over backward to be fair to Dan Kincade, perhaps she'd gone too far. If Calvin did have something to say that would indict his coach or the program at the college, he certainly wouldn't want to state his case in front of the man who could make or break his chances for a professional career.

''I realize you didn't know Coach Kincade would be here,'' she said hastily. ''If you'd like, Calvin, we can make this interview confidential.''

The young man's dark gaze moved slowly from Jonnie's face to Dan's and back again. ''No. I guess it's okay.''

''All right. If you're sure.'' Her voice still held a question.

''Why don't you just turn on your recorder and let him get it over with,'' Dan grated out between clenched teeth. He glanced down meaningfully at his watch. "I've still got a practice to conduct this afternoon, if we're not too busy saving the sports world from corruption."

Jonnie ignored his sarcasm, switching on the small desk tape recorder with its condenser mike. It was unobtrusive, but she noticed beads of sweat dotting the young man's forehead as he eyed it with all the nervousness he might a poisonous rattlesnake, poised to strike.

"Would you prefer a question-and-answer format? Or do you just want to tell your story your own way?" she asked softly, her tone intended to calm him.

Jonnie knew a tape recorder could be an unnerving third party in any interview, which was why she had chosen the compact, cigarette-pack size. She would have preferred to forgo the intrusion altogether, but the recorder protected her from being accused of misquoting and allowed her to direct her full attention to her subject.

"I think I'd just like to tell you how I see it," he mumbled, looking down at enormous hands that were twisting nervously in his lap. "How a lot of the guys see it...." He lifted his gaze to hers. "We know you mean well, Miss Ryan. And we know your dad was a great coach. But it's impossible for you to change anything. Because it's the system—not the coaches like Coach Kincade—who are to blame."

Jonnie nodded encouragingly. "Go on, Calvin."

She watched as his hands unfolded and rubbed self-consciously on his long denim-clad thighs.

"I grew up in the Hough area in Cleveland. There you didn't have a choice about whether you join a gang or not, Miss Ryan. It was survival, understand?"

Jonnie nodded.

"I was one of the lucky ones because I could play basketball. I could do dunks when I was twelve years old. Not one of the nine high schools that recruited me ever bothered to bring up academics. Not one."

"Did you ever ask?"

Calvin looked at Jonnie as if she were crazy, then his glance slid to Dan, as if to ask, hey, is this chick for real?

"No. Because I wasn't thinking education, ma'am, I was thinking pros." He leaned forward to make his point, his forearms braced on his thighs. "It's like an obsession. If you don't make it to the pros, your life is over."

"I hope you don't still believe that."

"Not anymore. But I sure as hell did."

Jonnie nodded. "Why don't you tell me what changed all that?"

"I was high-point man in high school. Every night I'd make thirty, thirty-five points. If I didn't, I couldn't face anyone. I was the Force. Everyone counted on me. I was someone to look up to...."

His face grew hard for a moment as he recalled those days. "I had friends, thirteen, fourteen years old doing strong-arm robberies. But I was a stud, understand? Because I could play the game.''

''I understand, Calvin.''

''Nobody ever made me work real hard for grades. It was like payment. Hey, kid, you get the team to the state finals and you'll get a B in algebra. It always made sense to me. I knew basketball stars made the big bucks. It only seemed right that the payments started early on.''

Jonnie couldn't argue with his reasoning, despite her distaste for a system that made it so.

''Then my economics teacher died, and we had a substitute for the rest of the year. He was going to flunk me for not showing up for class.''

''And?''

''The other teachers, they went and talked to the guy. They told him, 'Calvin's an athlete, understand? He's not going to be into books.' They explained it's hard to make a guy ineligible when he's packing our gym. I got my grade and everything was cool.''

''I see.''

''No. You don't see. A student athlete is different from the time he's out there doing playground ball. He never has to ask for anything. He gets it. His counselor's his coach, and he never becomes part of the student population. I thought about being a computer engineer for a while, designing those videogames, you know?''

Jonnie nodded, not wanting to interrupt as Calvin Dunn got more and more into his story.

"Well, I scored off the board in the tests, but I was the Force, you gotta understand. Can you imagine me telling the coach, 'Hey coach, I gotta skip practice because I'm working overtime in the lab'?" He gave a healthy snort. "What do you think any high school coach in the country would say?"

"I can tell you what I'd like him to say," she answered instead.

"Grow up, Miss Ryan. What do you think he'd say?" The words were out before the young man could retract them and his eyes widened with despair at his rudeness. She watched as his dark gaze cut to Dan, as if seeking help out of the pit he'd just dug for himself.

"That's all right, Calvin, I'm certain Miss Ryan didn't take that personally." Dan's deep voice held a trace of laughter, but his face was set in an inscrutable mask.

"Of course I didn't, Calvin," she agreed. "And I'm afraid you're right about the average coach's response. But that doesn't make it morally acceptable."

"That's what I'm trying to tell you. Look, as long as my eligibility held out I could get anything I wanted. I got free clothes, lunches. I even got a car."

"A car? In high school?" One russet brow rose disbelievingly.

"Sure. I was supposed to be working at a dealership, washing the cars on the lot every morning, that sort of thing. But everyone knew I didn't have time for that. We had early-morning practice. It just looked like I was buying the car out of my paychecks on paper. But I never soaped up one car or paid one cent.''

When he was convinced she believed him, he continued. ''I was recruited by every major university in the country. I had guys lay down ten, twelve thousand dollars on the table, asking me to sign. Hell, one time on a recruiting trip to see the campus I was even set up with a date.''

''Did all the colleges offer you money?'' she asked quietly, feeling Dan tense beside her.

Jonnie was unprepared for Calvin's burst of laughter. ''Not all. A few decided I wouldn't fit into their curriculum. They kinda like to have their jocks go to class, and I didn't look like a safe bet to make it through the first semester. They didn't want to blow the scholarship on a potential washout.... Then there was Cascades.''

He grinned over at Dan. ''Coach Kincade recruited me personally. He didn't even talk about the game. Just handed me a book and said 'read.' Then he accused me of having a transcript that could win the Pulitzer Prize for fiction.''

''Was it faked?''

''The transcript wasn't exactly. But,'' he said, his grin widening, ''the grades might have been slightly exaggerated. Coach Kincade told me that if I came here I'd have to agree to summer shool and tutoring the rest of the year. I was about ready to walk out. I was the Force, and he was treating me like I was some kinda snot-nosed failure.''

"And then?"

"Then he told me something I'll never forget. He stood up, shook my hand and wished me luck wherever I ended up. Then he said, 'Remember Calvin, what you are will affect whatever happens to you.' I sat back down and signed his damn paper."

The tape lacing its way through the magnetic heads was still whirring in the sudden silence of the room, and Jonnie leaned forward, turning it off.

"Thank you, Calvin." She rose, holding out her hand to the young man. "I know that whatever happens with your basketball career, you've got a good life ahead of you."

After he'd gone she turned to Dan. "That's true, isn't it? It's not some story hatched up to make you look like a crusading hero."

"You're the crusader, Ryan. Not me, remember?"

Jonnie's gaze was thoughtful as she studied his bland expression. "I think you're a phony, Dan Kincade. You insist my commission is off the track, yet you feel exactly the same way I do about the abuses in collegiate sports."

Jonnie now realized that her fears about Dan hiding something were ill-founded, and her relief made her feel like crying the news out from the rooftops. She'd be ending her investigation soon; then she could set about convincing Dan they shared more than a common interest in sports. That idea sent her spirits soaring to new heights.

Dan's harsh words brought her crashing back to earth with a jolt. "If you're talking about the fact that the system holds out athletic scholarships as a carrot to kids, pointing to the pros as the gold at the end of the rainbow, I agree it's a crime. If you're talking about the fact that high schools are set up to graduate student athletes, not educate them, I agree something needs to be done there. If you're referring to the fact that we turn them out into the world with few prospects except pro ball, I'd willingly be hung by my heels if I thought there was one case I'd participated in where that was true."

His eyes hardened, turning a blue crystal. "But, we'll never agree on the fact that your commission is the answer, Jonnie. Because you're not seeking answers, just indictments."

Jonnie's eyes roamed the ceiling as she fought for renewed patience. "What do I have to do to convince you that you're wrong about that?"

"Have dinner with me."

That brought her gaze abruptly back down to his face. They'd been working together all week, Dan readily supplying anything Jonnie had required. He'd kept things on a strictly business basis, and it had appeared that as long as she was investigating his school he had no intention of treating her as anything other than Jonnie Ryan, Counselor at Law. He'd been polite, but distant.

"Will that change your mind about my work?" she asked hopefully, knowing the answer beforehand.

"Hell, no. But it'll sure make my lonely evening a lot brighter. This isn't easy, Ryan, having you so close and yet so far. Every time you breeze into my office, all official and authoritative, it's all I can do to keep my mind on business. I want to lock that damn door, tell Janet and Kimberly no calls for a week and ravish you in every conceivable manner. And quite a few inconceivable ones, too."

"You've done a good job of hiding those urges, Dan. I was beginning to think I'd successfully blended into the furnishings around here."

"Not unless the furnishings have taken to wearing that enticing perfume you've got on right now."

He'd risen and come to stand within six inches of her uplifted face. His eyes were a dark indigo, and Jonnie knew her own desire was mirrored in those blue pools.

"I'm not wearing any perfume," she whispered, suddenly knowing how quicksand must feel as she was pulled deeper and deeper into his liquid gaze.

"See what I mean? You're getting under my skin, Jonnie. Because I can't get the sweet scent of you out of my mind."

"Dan—" Her soft eyes invited the kiss she'd been yearning for all week.

"Gotta get to practice, Ryan," he said abruptly, moving away with a chagrined shake of his head. He turned in the doorway, his hands in the pockets of his slacks. "Dinner," he reminded her. "I'll even find a place with brown bread and tofu."

Jonnie needed no enticement to be alone with Dan Kincade away from his athletic complex, which only served to emphasize their differences. Her words echoed her thoughts immediately.

"Not if you feel more like steak," she offered expansively, deciding she could always order a salad. "We could go to the Stein and Sirloin. I hear it's nice."

Dan laughed. "I wouldn't do that to you, Jonnie. Besides, I'm the one who's out of step. You know what they say about Eugene residents."

Jonnie grinned. "About only stopping their jogging long enough to eat their sprouts and check the air quality?"

"Got it," he agreed cheerfully. "To tell you the truth, I think you should just move down here permanently. You'd fit right in, babe."

Jonnie could feel her heart skip a beat. Had he meant it? Was he asking her to move down here to be with him, or was it general chitchat? She sighed as he left, returning to work. It must be the latter. If Dan was the slightest bit interested in any type of long-term relationship, he sure had a funny way of showing it.

It was late when Jonnie finished up her work and went to track Dan down. She knew that if he was running on schedule practice would be nearly over. She approached the gym, not hearing the usual thudding of the basketball against the parquet floor, the shrill whistle, or Dan's barked instructions. Entering the empty gymnasium, she stopped dead in her tracks, her words of greeting blocked in her throat.

The team had obviously gone to the showers. She could only assume the assistant coaches and trainer had been sent away by Dan. The man obviously desired privacy.

Her heart was doing horrible things as she watched him kissing the woman, his manner as warm and tender as it had ever been with her. The woman had her back to Jonnie, but even from this vantage point, it was easy to tell the petite figure was perfect. She was standing on tiptoe, her arms wrapped about Dan's neck, her shoulder-length chestnut hair a glossy sleek curtain skimming down her back. As Jonnie turned and escaped the room she heard the sound of laughter, one voice a silver melody, the other deep, husky and appreciative.

She gathered up her things as quickly as possible, intent on leaving the athletic building so she wouldn't have to face him again. If there was one thing she certainly didn't want to do, it was to be alone with him while his mind was on some other woman.

As she reached the parking lot, two things hit Jonnie simultaneously. First, if she just took off like this she'd have to explain her behavior. She could tell him she'd simply forgotten their date, but she knew Dan would never believe that. The second thought was that she'd already assured him she was a mature woman, not given to adolescent romantic fantasies. She could run now, but she'd only be wearing her heart on her sleeve by such a response. And he'd back away even further than he'd been this past week.

She certainly didn't want that. She'd have to pretend nothing at all had happened. As she walked slowly back to the office, Jonnie gave herself a brisk pep talk.

"Hi. All ready?"

Jonnie marveled at the degree of warmth in Dan's tone, considering the fact that moments before he'd been locked in an embrace with another woman.

"I suppose so. Where are we going?" She glanced down at her dress, as if to ask if it were appropriate attire.

"Home. I wandered over to the home economics department today, and Cheryl Brooks worked up a vegetarian meal she swears is delicious. I'd planned to stop on the way home, pick up the stuff and cook you a dinner you won't forget."

His grin was so self-satisfied that Jonnie didn't know whether to weep or hit the man over the head with the brass paperweight resting on the wide desk. How could he do it—have one of his women plan a seduction meal for another? Was she the one who was so badly out of step? Cheryl Brooks certainly hadn't seemed disturbed earlier when she'd delivered the menu.

"You don't have to do that," she snapped.

Dan's eyes narrowed as he studied her carefully. "I realize that. But you haven't left this room for more than a few minutes today. I thought I'd give you a chance to put your feet up and relax while I show you my hidden talents."

She'd already seen a few of those. The man had such a good juggling act going for himself that if he ever gave up basketball he could begin an entirely new career at Ringling Brothers.

"I'm certain you're just full of surprises," Jonnie said briskly, walking past him. "I'll see you at the house, then."

"Sure." He dug into his pocket, withdrawing a key ring. Sliding the house key off, he handed it to her. "Make yourself at home," he offered. "I'll only be a few minutes. Cheryl even listed the stores where I can pick up the ingredients."

"Cheryl sounds like an absolute gem," she murmured, taking the key from his outstretched hand and dropping it into her purse.

As Jonnie left, she felt Dan's puzzled scrutiny. She kept her head up, her shoulders squared and her stride long and purposeful. She could be every bit as nonchalant about this as that wonderful paragon of perfection, Cheryl Brooks.

"That was very good," she admitted reluctantly, hating at this point to give Dan Kincade credit for anything. But the manicotti, salad and herb bread had been delicious. If she hadn't known who planned the damn meal, she would've enjoyed her dinner immensely.

"It wasn't bad, was it?" he agreed, looking somewhat surprised. "Cheryl promised I wouldn't miss the meat. She also gave me a recipe for a soybean burger we'll try one of these days when I'm feeling a bit more adventurous.''

"You don't have to go out of your way for me."

"I like doing things for you, Jonnie."

His tone was so sincere, Jonnie couldn't stand it another minute. All during dinner they'd been carrying on an inane, chatty conversation, acting as if nothing was happening. Dan had been in a better mood than she'd seen him all week and she was loathe to determine whether it was the kiss he'd shared with Cheryl, or the prospect of an intimate dinner with her that made him so happy. His slightly off-key whistling had driven her up the wall, and she'd been forced to take a walk in the woods behind his house, seeking an excuse to escape the kitchen. She'd remained away as long as possible, only returning when a light rain began.

"Tell me about your friend Cheryl," she instructed, needing desperately to know about this woman—this rival.

Rival? Jonnie certainly couldn't lay claim to Dan Kincade. But she wanted to. Oh Lord, how badly she wanted to be a part of his life! More and more, as she'd watched his close relationship with the team, Jonnie was learning that Dan had a lot more going for him than good looks and a terrific smile. He was one of those individuals who really cared—about his players and, although she knew he wouldn't want to admit it, about her.

Despite the fact that another woman had planned this meal, it had been Dan who'd gone to the trouble of searching out a vegetarian menu. He'd shopped for the alien foodstuffs and then even cooked it for her, all because he believed she'd been working too hard.

A nice man, she determined, breathing a light sigh. A good man. And that's why she was slowly, inexorably, falling in love with him.

Dan appeared not to notice her distress and lifted his wide shoulders in a careless shrug. "There's not much to tell. She's a nice lady who decided for one reason or another it was up to her to make certain I don't starve. Most of the stuff in my freezer has been from assignments for term projects in her nutrition classes. She approves, by the way, of how you've modified your diet to allow dairy products and eggs."

Terrific. Not only did the woman have the inside track on being Dan's next girlfriend, she'd even thought ahead and stocked the pantry.

"It must be nice to have your friends take such a personal interest in you," she said with saccharine sweetnesss.

"I think she's lonely. She was widowed this year and doesn't have anyone to cook for. Being the lone bachelor on the faculty, I was elected."

"What happened? Isn't she a little young to be a widow?" Jonnie was curious in spite of herself at how a young woman who couldn't be more than twenty had managed to find herself in such a state.

"Young?" Dan refilled their wineglasses. "I've never thought about it. She's been teaching here twenty-five years, so she must be somewhere around fifty. I suppose that is a bit younger than you'd expect."

"But—" Jonnie's surprise was etched onto her face as she attempted to figure out where this conversation had gone astray.

Dan was there before her. "Uh-oh. You already had your coat on when I showed up at the office. Had you by chance been looking for me?"

At her tight face, he nodded, not needing an answer. "And you just happened by the gym at the precise time Ann Bishop was presenting me with that little token of her gratitude."

"Ann Bishop?" The name rang a bell and Jonnie's smooth forehead furrowed as she attempted to place it. When she did, it was an unpalatable revelation.

Dan caught the recognition. "Right. Brian Bishop's wife. The point guard with the terrific grades."

"I see."

"It's not what you think, you know." His voice was smooth and unruffled.

"Of course not."

"I did Ann a favor. She's an enthusiastic girl and that was her way of thanking me. That's all there is to it."

"I don't suppose you'd be willing to disclose just what type of favor you could have possibly done to encourage such gratitude?"

Dan rose from the table, clearing the dishes. "Nope. But it's nice to know you were jealous." The grin he flashed at her was so self-confident Jonnie felt like throwing the last of the manicotti at his head.

"I wasn't jealous at all."

"Sure you were," he countered, bending down to give her a quick, hard kiss. "Just as I would've been if I'd seen you locked in a clinch with some other guy. But you handled it beautifully, Jonnie. Some women would've been in there screaming and throwing things." His eyes were bright with admiration. "You're one cool cookie, Ryan."

Sure, Jonnie agonized, not knowing whether she felt better or worse. She didn't like him believing she could be so casual about an affair. It was one thing to pretend experience she didn't have, but another to actually live that way. How could he ever begin to take their relationship seriously if he didn't think she did? What a tangled web, she mused silently, gazing down into the red burgundy as if hoping to find the answer in the swirling depths.

"I'm going to miss you." Dan's voice registered regret as he walked her out to her car. "I suppose you have to go?"

"I have to. But just for the weekend," she said softly, leaning back against the car door as she looped her hands about his lean waist. "I'll be back Monday," she offered hopefully.

"You know we leave on a road trip Monday afternoon," he complained, his fingers tracing her slim jawline, then her lips.

Jonnie kissed his fingertips lightly. "Do you think the busy Coach Kincade will be available for an interview Monday morning?"

"I'll be available," he promised, opening the car door for her reluctantly. "And Jonnie—"

"Yes?" She stopped in the motion of buckling her seat belt, looking up into the tender blue eyes.

"Take care of yourself. I worry about you driving on those slippery roads."

Jonnie fought down her surge of disappointment. She'd been hoping for some intimate confession. Well, she'd gotten one all right, but it still sounded more like something a man might say to his little sister. She sighed.

"I'll be careful," she murmured, deciding it would do little good to belabor the fact that she was all grown up. She'd just have to keep working to prove it to him.

Dan grinned with masculine satisfaction. "That's my girl."

He closed her car door and stood with his hands thrust deep into his pockets, his face becoming hard as he watched her drive away. Tomorrow, he knew, she'd be reporting back to William Murdock, and then she'd discover it was not going to be as simple as she believed. Dan was beginning to realize he'd misjudged her. But he knew Murdock was determined to rise to fame from the ashes of Dan Kincade's funeral pyre. And it mattered little to the politician if he destroyed the college's entire athletic program in the bargain.

Chapter Six

"What in the hell do you call this?"

William Murdock flung the manila folder across his immaculate mahogany desk, causing a flurry of papers to spill out onto the soft-beige carpeting.

Jonnie's eyes followed the path of fallen papers, and she shook her head in confusion. A few errant curls escaped the neat topknot, adding a note of whimsy to her otherwise serious image. She was back in her working clothes, her suit neat and unadorned, her hair forced into what she considered a more professional style.

"It's the initial results of my investigation," she said.

William Murdock, chairman of the Murdock Commission, undeclared candidate for state attorney general and Jonnie's boss and mentor, only glared in response. His brown eyes were dark and accusing as a long, perfectly manicured finger jabbed the air in her direction.

"And just what do you suggest I do with all this Pollyanna gibberish?"

"Present it to the commission," she answered promptly. "I'd think everyone would be pleased to know that the College of the Cascades, for one, appears to be operating on the straight and narrow."

"Pleased?" His voice hit a higher pitch than his usual oratorical tone. "Ryan, you're not a newcomer to politics. Dammit, you should know better than that."

She rubbed her palms surreptitiously on her skirt. She had the uneasy feeling she could predict what William was getting around to, and she didn't like the premonitions skimming up her spine like icy fingers.

"Perhaps you'd better explain this in more detail, William," she suggested softly.

William stopped pacing the floor for a moment, spearing her with a sharp gaze. His hands were deep in the front pockets of his gray slacks, the European-cut jacket pushed back. He was, she noted, not for the first time, a vibrantly attractive man. It was difficult to imagine any woman being able to cast a vote against him. He was tall, with wavy chestnut hair and hooded eyes the color of rich dark chocolate. Under normal conditions a woman would have to be asleep not to feel some attraction for him.

But these were not normal circumstances, she realized, watching his dark eyes circle the room before returning to study her intently.

"We've worked together a long time, Jonnie." His voice softened as he perched on the corner of his desk, his body inclined toward her. His expression was one of an indulgent friend, and he'd recovered the deeptimbred voice. It rang from the gleaming paneled walls, filling the room with his baritone.

"A long time," Jonnie agreed, nodding her head. "My entire career in the law has been spent working with you in one capacity or another, William. You know I appreciate all you've done for me."

While Jonnie certainly wasn't as close to William Murdock as certain gossip mongers had so cruelly intimated, he had been the driving force behind her upwardly mobile career. She'd met him when she was still in law school and he'd come to lecture to a class she was taking on legislative lawmaking. He was a charismatic, forceful speaker, and Jonnie had been thrilled to find herself invited, along with two other topranked students, to a small reception in his honor.

That evening he'd taken Jonnie aside, the two of them escaping for a time into an office in the dean's home where the reception was being held. They'd talked about the power of politics and law for over an hour. At the end of that conversation he'd invited Jonnie to join his campaign and she had, unhesitatingly. For five years she'd worked for him in a variety of positions. His arranging her appointment to his commission only demonstrated how much he respected her judgment and ability. It was not, as some columnists had insinuated, because they were intimate.

He drew his brows into a warning frown. "We won't accomplish a thing if all we do is spend the taxpayers' money to inform them that Daniel Kincade and his fellow coaches are nice guys. Everyone who's ever picked up a sports page knows that, Jonnie. What we need is some dirt. The facts."

She thought briefly about what Dan had said about rules and fairness and used the form of his question to her boss.

"And what if dirt and the facts aren't always the same thing?"

He moved around behind the desk, sitting down in his dark leather chair, leaning back as he wore an aura of supreme self-confidence.

"No one's perfect, Jonnie. Not even Boy Scouts like Kincade. He's bound to have violated the rules somewhere—recruiting, transcripts, payoffs. All we need is one little slip and we're on our way."

"I don't think I'm going to find anything, William. I know Dan Kincade. I've known him since I was a child. If Diogenes had met him, he could've put down his lantern and given up his search for an honest man."

William expelled a weary, exaggerated sigh. "If you're so up on Greek philosophers, Ryan, don't forget this one from Demosthenes: 'For what each man wishes, that he also believes to be true.' Is it possible you're entering into this investigation wearing rose-colored glasses because Kincade is an old friend?''

"Of course not," she answered swiftly. "I've been working very hard, William. I've gone through the first batch of records with a fine-tooth comb, and there's absolutely nothing there to discredit Dan Kincade or the college."

"Well, get back there and keep digging," he advised. "Nobody's this clean, Jonnie. There's no such thing as a perfectly honest man."

"All right," she said softly. "But I still say you're wrong on this one."

Her undergraduate degree in philosophy had not been forgotten. As Jonnie rose from the chair, moving toward the door, she recalled one of the old maxims: "He *who says* there *is* no such thing *as an honest man,* you *may be sure is* himself *a* knave." George Berkeley, *Maxims Concerning Patriotism.* She secretly marked down one point for her side.

"Ryan?"

She turned, eyeing him over her shoulder. "Yes?"

"I've been around a lot longer than you. There's something there. You just have to keep digging until you hit pay dirt." He smiled with all the warmth of a hungry shark. "You might try a different, time-honored technique for a change."

"And what's that?"

"You're an attractive woman, Jonnie. Dan Kincade is a man. You figure it out."

Jonnie reddened with an angry flush. "That's a horrible thing to suggest, William."

He shrugged, turning his attention to gathering up the scattered pages of her initial report. "Hell, honey, those methods go back further than Mata Hari. And they might prove effective. Men have been known to tell a lot of secrets while enjoying some relaxation in a warm bed with a willing woman."

"She wouldn't do it. I know she wouldn't."

Dan Kincade was awkwardly slumped in the vinyl chair, his tall frame ill-designed for the traditionally styled office furniture. His forearms rested along the wooden arms of the chair; his long legs stretched far out in front of him. But the pained look on his face was not due to any physical discomfort.

E.G. Harrison, athletic director at the College of the Cascades, responded by shaking his head and tapping the folded newspaper with a pencil.

"Where do you suppose they got this? Not from me. And certainly not from you."

Dan's dark gaze moved reluctantly to the headline, a muscle jumping in his cheek. "I don't know," he admitted.

"It had to be her. That's the only answer. I tell you, the woman's dynamite, and she's got the capacity of taking us all up with her when she blows."

Although Dan had been telling himself precisely that same thing from the moment Jonnie had walked into his office, all professionally correct and undeniably beautiful, he didn't want to accept it. Despite the fact that he was still having problems separating the desirable woman from the little girl he'd known and loved, he wanted Jonnie Ryan more than he'd ever wanted any woman in his life.

But it wasn't mere lust; she filled every pocket of his mind with her presence. During practice, he thought about her beautiful smile and was hard pressed to maintain the strict discipline that had become his trademark. He remembered the sweet taste of her lips when he went over the next year's recruiting prospects with his assistant coaches and could have agreed to sign a five-foot center for all the attention he paid to the scouting reports.

He pictured those warm, full lips smiling at him the moment he woke up in the morning, and she stayed with him throughout the day until he viewed her soft sea-green eyes before finally falling to sleep. And even then he was haunted by her gently curved body, her throaty laugh and her touch that could turn his body into an intense fireball threatening to blaze out of control at any moment.

He didn't want to have to consider Jonnie Ryan, the professional politician who was out to build a name for her boss. He didn't want to remind himself that she had flown up the ladder of political success since leaving college, achieving every single thing she'd aimed for. He was loathe to believe she was so ambitious she would bulldoze over him to further her own career.

The tapping of the graphite point on the damning black headline drew his attention back to the matter at hand. It didn't look good for any of them right now, whoever was to blame.

"Be careful, Dan," Harrison warned softly. "I've more to consider than our friendship. If the Ryan girl manages to uncover that little incident with Bishop, I'm going to have to back away in a professional capacity. It was a personal decision on your part, and I'll have to declare it as such. I don't always agree with the limitations put on the athletic programs, but rules are rules. The team could end up on probation if the truth of what you did gets out. And I don't have to tell you the straits the college would be in if we lost the television revenues. I owe it to the college to look at the larger picture."

His gray eyes held the bleak ones of the younger man. E.G. Harrison liked Dan Kincade and respected him as a player, a coach, and a man. But respect was not the issue at the moment.

Dan heaved a sigh, unfolding his long length from the low chair. He held his hand out toward the athletic director.

"Don't worry, E.G., I understand. I wouldn't want anything to happen to Cascades due to me." He thrust his jaw out a little, and squared his shoulders, no longer looking like a naughty young boy called into the principal's office. "I'd do it again, you know."

Harrison rose, put his arm around Dan's shoulder and walked him to the door. "I know, Dan. And that's why, whatever happens, you've got my heartfelt admiration.''

Terrific, Dan considered, steering the Blazer around the rain-slicked curves of the hilly roadway to his home. *I could end up admired and unemployed.* And the unbelievable thing about this entire mess was that his future was in the hands of a woman who'd already disrupted his life more than he'd ever thought possible.

Jonnie drove over the slippery roads toward Eugene, returning a day earlier than planned. She wanted more time with Dan before his road trip. By the time she had driven thirty miles, she'd calmed down and was no longer upset by William's accusations. She'd always known he saw things more cynically than she, but it had never bothered her before. This time, however, someone she loved was involved. And she did love Dan. Not with the schoolgirl crush she'd had through the rosy haze of adolescence, but with a mature love, coupled with respect.

She also knew with an iron-clad certainty that he would never do anything illegal or even dishonest. And when her investigation was over and she moved on to the next school, William Murdock and the entire state of Oregon would know it, too.

Loving thoughts of Dan caused her mind to wander pleasantly. Suddenly, her back wheels spun as she tried to maneuver a tight curve in the road, and although she jerked her mind back to reality, her efforts came too late. The car swung to the outside and Jonnie felt the right wheels sinking into the mud on the soft shoulder.

She kicked the tire with frustration as she viewed it stuck in the dark red mud up to the hubcap. Now what? Glaring up at the slate sky, which was still dropping water onto the Willamette Valley, she knew that there would be little traffic on the road circling the wooded park today. She had no choice but to start walking.

Dan's eyes opened wide, his gaze shooting past her, searching for her car as he observed her shivering on his doorstep.

"Jonnie, what in the hell . . . ?"

"I had to come early. I wanted you all to myself before you left."

His eyes narrowed, taking in her soaked appearance, as he beckoned her into the warmth of his house.

"Where's your car? I didn't hear you drive up."

She shook her head, giving a slightly self-deprecating grin. This was certainly dandy evidence that she was a mature, capable woman.

"It's down the hill. I slid off the roadway."

Jonnie was startled by the way Dan grabbed her shoulders, his gaze raking down her body. "Were you hurt?"

"Of course not. I just got stuck in a little mud, that's all. Tomorrow I'll have the motor club pull me out."

He made a grunt that indicated he was not at all concerned with her car. "I knew you shouldn't be commuting. It's too damn dangerous."

Jonnie's eyes softened as they roamed the harsh contours of his face. "Hey, Kincade, settle down. I'm fine. Besides, I'm not really commuting. I'm back for as long as it takes."

"What takes?"

Was that white line around his lips caused by fear for her safety, or anger? She reached up, brushing at it with her fingertips.

"A lot of things," she murmured. "My work, for one." She didn't add that she was determined to convince Dan that a lasting relationship between them was possible once they put the investigation behind them.

"We need to talk about that," he growled, pulling her over to the couch. "Do you want something to drink? Scotch? Wine? Brandy?"

"At nine in the morning?"

Was it still that early? He'd retrieved his paper from the bushes at six-thirty. At seven he'd been in the office of the athletic director. The time since then had seemed like hours, as he'd been forced to seriously question Jonnie's involvement in the indicting press release.

"I've been told I underestimated you, Jonnie."

Jonnie shivered again, as much from sudden fear as chill. There was something cold and distant in his expression, something she hadn't seen before.

"I don't understand, Dan."

"Maybe a little show and tell is in order." He left the room, returning a moment later with the front page of the Sunday paper, which he thrust at her. "There—I've shown. Now why don't you tell me exactly where this came from."

Jonnie forced her eyes to focus on the damning headline. MURDOCK COMMISSION TO BREAK SILENCE. The article was a series of inflammatory lies. Jonnie's blood ran cold as she read the innuendos. Alleging that secret funds were soon to be exposed, an unnamed reliable source promised to "blow athletic circles sky-high," with news of slush funds and recruiting scandals.

She dropped the paper from her lifeless fingers, and it fell to the floor with a heavy thud.

"Dan, I didn't . . . I'm not responsible. . . ."

His narrowed eyes moved over her face with agonizing slowness, searching out secrets hidden within her soul. "You don't know how I want to believe that, Jonnie."

Unconsciously, with the tip of her tongue, Jonnie circled lips which were becoming unbearably dry. Dan's gaze moved to her mouth, following her nervous gesture. She saw the flares sparking his cobalt eyes and knew it was not anger Dan was feeling for her at this moment.

"I would never leak anything like that to the press, Dan. It's not even the truth! I've already told William that I don't expect to find anything here that even hints at wrongdoing."

That seemed to get his attention as his eyes jerked back to hers, holding her gaze with unnerving intensity. "What did he say to that?"

"He thinks I'm naive. He swears there's no such thing as an honest man. But I know you, Dan. And I'd never do anything that underhanded." Her hand gestured toward the paper lying at their feet, but her eyes never moved from his probing gaze.

Suddenly, her soft protest was smothered as his mouth silenced hers savagely. There was a strong element of anger in Dan's kiss as his hot, ravenous lips ground against her mouth, and through her swirling senses Jonnie realized Dan was releasing his frustration both at her and their situation. Jonnie knew she was being punished for upsetting Dan Kincade's nice little world, the world where he had everything under control exactly to his liking.

The knowledge should have caused her to hate the lips plundering the tender fullness of her own, devouring her with a burning, insatiable male hunger. But there was something in the flood of emotions behind this silent combat that caused a furious heat to spiral outward from her very core. When his tongue thrust into the dark, secret corners of her mouth, her own leaped up to meet it, tangling in sensuous battle. Jonnie flung her arms about his neck and clung to him shamelessly, her full breasts crushed by his chest. She fell back onto the cushions of the couch, pulling Dan with her, every nerve singing in heightened response as he fitted himself against her.

Jonnie's hands skimmed freely over the hard muscle of him, inciting him to greater intimacies. She loved Dan Kincade and right now she wanted him with every atom of her being. She moved sinuously against him, kindling the flames between their heated bodies.

Dan slid his hands up along her thighs, the heat of his touch threatening to burn off the soaked jeans clinging to her legs. He pressed his palm against her in a caress that had her moaning in ragged desire as she returned the intimate gesture in kind.

"Wanton," he groaned, dragging his lips finally from hers and raining his own shower of kisses over her face. "I swore I wouldn't do this," he whispered hoarsely. "God knows I've tried to keep my hands off you, Jonnie."

He sucked in a harsh breath as she ran her fingernails up the metal track of his zipper. "My God! You're just as forward as you were in the old days, Jonnie Ryan."

Jonnie feathered kisses on his eyelids, his nose, the deep cleft of his chin. Dear Lord, how she loved this man!

"No, I'm worse," she admitted openly. "I'm not going to run home and cry this time, Dan. I want you too much."

Dan's blue eyes blazed surrender and conquest simultaneously. "I don't know which of us is the crazier," his deep voice rumbled against her temple as he pressed his lips upon her beating pulse point. "But for now, I'm willing to give up trying to figure it out."

Chapter Seven

Dan shook his head, pulling back to give her a slanted grin. "The more things change..." he murmured, more to himself than to her.

"The more they stay the same," she finished softly, referring to how much she loved and wanted Dan Kincade.

His gaze traveled over her figure. "Not precisely the same."

He enveloped her hands in his, lifting her to her feet, handily lifting the damp wool sweater over her head. Next he knelt, freeing her of the wet suede boots. The first bark-brown boot slid off easily and his hands cupped her foot as she braced herself by holding onto his shoulders. His thumbs rubbed circles at her ankles, then he slid his hands under her jeans, moving up the curved fullness of her calf until his caress was impeded by the tight material. Jonnie shiv-

AN IMPORTANT MESSAGE FROM THE EDITORS

Dear Reader,

Because you've chosen to read one of our fine romance novels, we'd like to say "thank you"! And, as a **special** way to thank you, we've selected three more of the books you love so well, **and** a Free Picture Frame to send you absolutely FREE!

Please enjoy them with our compliments...

Editor,
The Best of the Best

P.S. And because we value our customers, we've attached something extra inside ...

EDITOR'S
FREE
GIFT
SEAL
THANK YOU

PEEL OFF SEAL AND PLACE INSIDE

HOW TO VALIDATE YOUR EDITOR'S FREE GIFT "THANK YOU"

1. Peel off gift seal from front cover. Place it in space provided at right. This automatically entitles you to receive three free books and a lovely Picture Frame decorated with celestial designs.

2. Send back this card and you'll get 3 of "The Best of the Best™" novels. These books have a cover price of $4.50 each, but they are yours to keep absolutely free.

3. There's no catch. You're under no obligation to buy anything. We charge nothing—ZERO—for your first shipment. And you don't have to make any minimum number of purchases—not even one!

4. We call this line "The Best of the Best" because each month you'll receive the best books by the world's hottest romance authors. These are authors whose names show up time and time again on all the major bestseller lists and whose books sell out as soon as they hit the stores. You'll love getting them conveniently delivered to your home...and you'll love our discount prices.

5. We hope that after receiving your free books you'll want to remain a subscriber. But the choice is yours—to continue or cancel, anytime at all! So why not take us up on our invitation, with no risk of any kind. You'll be glad you did!

6. Don't forget to detach your FREE BOOKMARK. And remember... just for validating your Editor's Free Gift Offer, we'll send you FOUR MORE gifts, *ABSOLUTELY FREE!*

YOURS FREE!

*This lovely Picture Frame is decorated with celestial designs — stars, moons and suns! It's perfect for displaying photographs of that "special someone" in your life and it's sure to please! And here's the best part: the frame is yours **absolutely free**, simply for accepting our no-risk offer!*

ered, not with chill but with expectation. Dan quickly began removing her wet clothing, and the other boot joined its mate on the floor.

He rose again, his long fingers unfastening the snaps at her waist, and lowering the zipper, he slid the soaked denim jeans down over her hips where they fell in a damp pile at her feet. Jonnie's head swam dizzily as Dan drew her into the cradle of his thighs, pressing her against him, molding her pliant female form to his hard frame.

"You were soaked all the way through," he murmured.

His breath was a gentle breeze against her skin as Dan's lips brushed little flickering tongues of fire along her shoulder, treating the lightly scattered freckles to a sensuous torment.

"I seem to be." Jonnie combed her fingers through his thick ebony curls and kissed the pulse spot throbbing wildly at the base of his throat. "But so are you. I'm sorry I got you wet, Dan. It was very thoughtless of me."

"I didn't notice."

She smiled in sweet concern. "It's a good thing I did. We can't have the coach catching cold."

Taking hold of the bottom of his sweater, she rose on her toes, pulling it over his head. Dan helped, and in a moment the dark-blue sweater dropped atop her own sodden clothing. When her hands moved to his belt, Dan covered them with his own, forestalling her progress.

"My turn."

His fingers traced the wide scalloped edging of her lacy bra, tugging it down a bit to expose the full curve of her breast and the soft coloring of freckles that dusted her creamy skin.

Jonnie had often quoted that old maxim—Oregonians don't tan, they rust—when bemoaning the fact that her soft skin would never darken to a deep golden hue. It did, however, possess the creaminess of gardenia petals, a perfect foil for her vibrant hair and soft-green eyes. At the moment a pink flush was glowing under the surface of her flesh, and Jonnie knew from the heated gleam in Dan's eyes that he had thus far not found her wanting.

"This is much better," he avowed with a deep growl, smothering her soft fullness with warm, wet kisses.

"What's much better?" Jonnie was grateful for the strong hands spanning her waist. She wasn't certain she was capable of standing on her own weak legs.

"Your freckles." Dan's tongue danced out to tantalize all her nerve endings, a heated rose color darkening the skin he explored. "I still love them. But hidden this way, I've got them all to myself."

"Dan...." Jonnie didn't know how much more of this sweet, tantalizing torment she could take as he slowly slid one satin ribbon strap down her arm.

His eyes burned as he lifted his gaze to hers, silently promising a world of sensual delights.

"You always were in a hurry, Jonnie Ryan," he teased, toying with the other strap until she thought she'd scream. Finally his fingers moved in the shadowed valley between her breasts, unfastening the front closure, leisurely divesting her of the lacy garment as if unwrapping the most special of presents. Now she stood clad only in the wispy bikini panties, welcoming his appraisal.

"So much woman," he murmured huskily, the flame rising even higher in his admiring eyes. "And every inch a beauty."

Jonnie felt neither embarrassment nor shame as Dan's compelling blue gaze moved over the contours of her body. She felt only that inner glow a woman experiences when a man—that certain, special man—finds her desirable. She smiled a warm, womanly smile. Jonnie had waited fifteen years for this moment, and now that it had arrived she wanted to make the most of it. She longed to draw every blissful moment out as long as physically possible.

"I think I'd like a warm shower," she declared, moving toward the stairway.

"To take the chill off," Dan agreed instantly, following her without hesitation.

Jonnie found the master bedroom without any problem, trying to hold back the tremor of anticipation that rippled up her spine as she passed Dan's king-sized bed. She slid the opaque-glass shower doors open, reaching in to turn on the water. When she'd stepped out of the brief panties, she turned to discover she'd lost Dan. Peeking around the doorframe, she saw him squatting before the roman-tile brick of yet another fireplace, striking a match against the rough stone of the hearth.

"You're getting behind," she scolded lightly.

"Just turning up the heat, babe," he answered, rising to face her. His hands moved to his belt and the light in his eyes was a gleaming promise.

"And here I thought you'd done that just fine already," she murmured.

She returned to the shower, her face uplifted to the brisk needles of warm water.

"About time." Jonnie held her arms out in welcome as Dan joined her.

"Woman, someone has to teach you to take your time," Dan muttered, shaking his dark black head with feigned chagrin. "You've been rushing headlong into things since the day I met you. And you haven't changed a bit."

Jonnie chose not to answer. Instead she reached out and took a bottle from a shelf in the corner of the shower, pouring the fragrant shampoo into the center of her palm. Tilting back her head, she massaged the lather into her thick auburn hair, her posture femininely provocative. She might be pretending to ignore Dan, but they both knew every movement was designed to be a sensuous invitation.

"Nothing's changed?" she challenged, her eyes closed as she allowed the water to stream through her thick mane. A moment later she was rewarded by the bar of soap being rubbed over her taut breasts and down her stomach.

"Tease," Dan growled, the pressure increasing as he moved the slippery rectangle down between her legs with a silky touch, spreading the luminous bubbles over her like a velvet cape.

When Jonnie's body threatened to melt beneath his hands, she took the soap from Dan and treated him to a similar form of ecstasy. She moved the soap over the firm hard muscles of his chest and down his flat stomach, following the arrowing of thick black hair. She knelt before him, the white soap held between her palms, moving down the firm pillars of his legs.

Jonnie glanced upward when she heard his short intake of breath and viewed Dan. His eyes were closed, the lush lashes thick and black against his cheeks. She saw, as well as heard, the thick moan issuing from the tanned column of his throat as she continued her sensual caresses, taking him in her soap softened hands.

The moan became an inarticulate, low growl. Dan's head was resting against the gold and toast-hued tile, his fingers tangling in her heavy, wet hair as Jonnie treated him to a torture so sweet, so prolonged, that she could feel the shudder of his body under her fingertips.

"Enough, woman." His hands moved to her shoulders as his eyes flew open, the fire nearly blazing out of control.

Dan lifted her back up, holding her face in his palms as he gazed into her love-softened eyes. As he searched her uptilted face, Jonnie knew he could read every loving emotion emblazoned on her features.

As they left the bathroom, the air was cool on her bare flesh, but Dan sat down on the bed, bringing her to lie beside him. Soon the combination of the crackling fire and his stroking hands warmed her to the boiling point. Jonnie's head was swimming with escalating desire, but not so much that she wasn't aware of a myriad of erotic sensations.

The crisp, chocolate-brown sheets were cool against her back as she twisted under Dan's ravishing touches. His feather caresses explored her ivory skin, skin that glowed in the golden flame of the fragrant cedar fire. Each succeeding touch of his hands and lips as they roamed her naked flesh caused her own fire to flame higher, and Jonnie moved against him, returning touch for touch, kiss for passionate kiss.

His crisp jet chest hairs were like springy little wires against her breasts, replaced by the softer curls of his head. The unwelcome beginning to his morning had caused Dan to forgo shaving, and when his beard scraped a provocative path along the inside of her thighs, it was as if the flames sparking in the fireplace had leaped the confines of the hearth and had flared dangerously out of control. They were caught up in the windswept inferno, and Jonnie moaned in exquisite torment, urging his head back up to enable her to drink from his lips.

Allowing her last conscious thought to flee, Jonnie was aware of nothing but Dan as she yielded to him, giving of herself with the same incendiary force he brought to their lovemaking. Entwined, they moved to the wondrous rhythm, consummating their feverish desire with a flare that became a united white-hot fireball.

Jonnie felt warm sparking currents moving through her body, and she sighed, luxuriating in Dan's strong embrace. Her breathing was still uneven, her long satiny legs entwined with even longer, hair-brushed ones.

Dan could not have made love to her like that unless he really did love her, Jonnie mused, delighting in her contented state. She knew it deep in her heart. She knew if she waited, biding her time patiently, Dan would come to realize that fact for himself. For now— well, she had enough love for both of them.

"God, you're wonderful." His lips grazed her ear with lazy kisses.

Jonnie's arms tightened about him, her body exulting in the feel of the muscular strength pressed against her soft curves.

"You're pretty terrific yourself," she answered, forcing her throaty, love-softened voice to a light tone.

Dan lifted his head, looking down into her soft-green eyes with a slow, studied appraisal. "No regrets?" A black brow lifted inquisitively over a crystal-blue eye.

Jonnie shook her head, smiling a warm, fully satisfied feminine smile. "Not a one," she answered honestly. She didn't regret a moment of their love-making.

"Wonderful," he repeated, his lips brushing hers as his hands moved up and down her body from her shoulder to her thigh. "You are one amazing woman, Jonnie Ryan."

Jonnie lost herself once again in the increasingly intimate kiss. It wasn't an undying declaration of love he'd just offered her. But his lips were telling her more than his words would allow.

"Dan?" Jonnie's fingers made little trails through the black forest carpeting his bare chest. "We need to talk."

"I think that's what I said when I invited you in," he agreed. His hands continued to trace her full, lush curves. "Think you can keep your mind on official business now?"

He was only teasing, his deep voice laced with self-amusement, but Jonnie knew they couldn't simply overlook the problem.

"Do you remember the Madison trial?" she asked softly.

He rolled over onto his back, pillowing his head with his arms as he looked toward her, obviously surprised by her apparent change in topics.

"Of course I do. It was only Oregon's biggest white-collar-crime trial in fifty years. I read about how well you handled your prosecution duties. How long did Madison get for all those counts of real-estate fraud?"

"Twenty-eight years," she answered distractedly. "But it's not the trial I want to talk about, Dan."

"You brought it up, babe," he reminded her gently.

"I know. I'm just trying to work my way up to the hard stuff."

He fell silent, his gaze on her as his long fingers brushed some tumbled hair back from her face. The tenderly intimate gesture almost caused her to weep.

"There was press from all over the country, all camped on the courthouse steps covering that trial. There was one reporter from the Phoenix *Herald-Examiner* who was particularly interested, since he'd covered a variety of land-fraud cases in Arizona. He'd taken a leave of absence to work on a book about the subject."

Dan sensed immediately where this conversation was headed. "Jonnie, you don't have to explain anything. Lord, I never expected you to be a virgin at your age, babe. And I haven't exactly been a saint, myself."

She shook her head, placing her fingers over his lips. "That's not why I'm telling you about Michael."

"Michael?" As he asked it, Dan wondered why in the hell he cared what the guy's name was. What did it matter?

"Michael Cunningham. I knew it was wrong to get involved with someone I worked with. But I never told him anything that wasn't cleared to be released to all the media. I knew I'd never compromise the trial for emotional reasons."

Dan thought about that for a moment, wondering if she'd compromise an investigation. He couldn't get a handle on Jonnie Ryan. She was too complex an individual. On one hand she seemed the paragon of the modern career woman: aggressive, single-minded, equality at all costs. The type Joan Crawford played on all the late movies. On the other hand, she was so soft and loving she made a man feel he could curl up in her arms and be safe forever.

"Anyway," she continued, missing the furrowing of his brow as he considered the weighty problem, "the trial lasted three months. Michael and I were together the last month."

"Jonnie, I still don't understand what this has to do with us," Dan protested, unnerved by the fact that he hated this Michael Cunningham, a man he'd never even met. What in the world was Jonnie Ryan doing to him?

"I know now I never loved him, but to be perfectly honest, it was so nice. I was working practically around the clock, and having someone to come home to was comforting."

Jonnie was taking her time with this story and Dan still didn't know what the guy had done to cause that sad expression shadowing her eyes. But he knew that if he ever had an opportunity he'd flatten the reporter for causing her pain. Which was a hell of a thought coming from the guy who could hurt her just as badly as she was threatening to hurt him.

"The one thing Michael forgot to mention was that there was Mrs. Cunningham back in Phoenix."

"You're kidding."

She stared into the embers of the fireplace, the coals a rich orange-and-red glow. "No, Michael was definitely married. The strange thing was what happened when I confronted him with it."

"He didn't deny it."

Jonnie turned toward him, her eyes wide, as if surprised he'd guessed so easily. "He didn't. What's more, he never could understand why I was so upset about his neglecting to tell me. He always assumed I was furious about his being married. He could never understand I was more upset about his living that lie."

"Would you have slept with him if you'd known?"

"Of course not. But that's not the point...." She took a deep breath, sitting up on the bed, her legs tucked under her, looking at him soberly. "I can't abide people who lie, Dan, for whatever reasons. There's never any good to come of it, and it only ends up hurting someone."

It was a struggle, but Dan kept his face composed as he met her intent gaze. "That's a hard line to hold, honey."

"I probably am too hard on others." Her slim, naked shoulders lifted in a slight shrug. "But I'm just as hard on myself. And that's why you have to know that I'd never give the paper those false statements." Her hand came out to rest on his arm. "I know you'll believe me, Dan, because you're the same way. Honest to a fault."

Damn it all to hell, Dan considered, viewing her serious expression. *This thing just keeps getting worse by the minute.* He gave up trying to come up with a solution and followed his instincts instead.

"You're a real special lady, Ryan," he murmured, holding the back of her head as his lips covered hers.

Chapter Eight

"Come in, Miss Ryan." Dan rose from behind his desk, moving toward the door in long strides.

"Why, thank you, Coach Kincade. I don't mind if I do." Jonnie's smile could have burned away all the clouds hovering over the city.

"Is there something I can do for you?" Dan locked the office door, turning to her with a pleasant leer.

"Yes, there is indeed, Coach Kincade." She held out her arms. "You can kiss me goodbye before you get on that horrid plane that's going to take you away from me."

"Only for five days."

Dan wrapped her in his strong arms, pulling her against him with a gentle force. They'd spent all of the previous day and the early hours of that morning making love, laughing, and delighting in the pleasure they found in each other's company. Although it had never been brought up, Dan knew it was by mutual consent they'd avoided any talk about her work at the college. She'd obviously put it out of her mind for the day because she had no worries in that regard. Dan had forced it from his mind because it could only poison what was, strangely enough, the first real enjoyment he'd gotten from anyone's company since those years living in that loving asylum the Ryans had called home. With five grown men and one young woman who could match every male Ryan for determination and lung power, the noise level in the hallways of the rambling three story house probably had surpassed recommended noise pollution levels.

There was always someone eating, always someone shouting for quiet while trying to talk on the phone and always two or three Ryans engaged in some type of contest. They were a happy, boisterous, competitive bunch, and while he'd at first been overwhelmed, he had learned to love them.

The thought had occurred to Dan sometime in the predawn hours of the morning that he needed to talk to Tom Ryan. Tom would understand what Dan had done, and while he might not have any clear-cut answers, at least he'd know how to break it to his daughter.

This relationship, which had been headed toward disaster from the beginning, had added one more fatal twist with Jonnie's little speech about honesty. Not only would she end up hating him on a professional basis, she'd be bound to turn away from him as a person. Dan had never cared how a woman felt about him before. He'd always done his best to be as charming as possible, a thoughtful and expert lover, but his previously nomadic life-style had not encouraged long-lasting relationships. If Jonnie felt him unworthy of her affection, it would be incredibly painful for him. Dan knew that instinctively.

"I hate the idea of your flying, Dan. I don't want to lose you." Her thin voice was muffled as she buried her head in his shoulder.

Jonnie had experienced the nightmare again, during the brief hours given up to sleep this morning. She hadn't had it for years. She'd been only eighteen months old when the commercial jetliner, on its approach to the runway, had plummeted to the ground after colliding with a private plane. She couldn't remember being pulled from the wreckage of the plane crash that had taken her mother's life. Even with counseling, she'd never been able to recall details. But her young mind had stored away images. Sights and sounds and scents that had contributed to the nightmares she'd experienced often in her younger years.

"I forgot."

Dan knew the story of Jonnie's past. He'd even comforted her after a few of those long-ago nightmares. His voice was grim as he stroked her hair.

"Jonnie, do you realize how many people fly every year in this country?"

"I know all that." Her mumbled answer was only absorbed by the winter-weight wool of his jacket. "I know that it's more dangerous to drive to the grocery store, climb up on a stepladder to change a light bulb or to take a bath. But, damn it, I still don't know how I'm going to stand it, thinking of you on that plane."

He sighed, his breath fanning her auburn hair. "Do you remember when you were ten? That first Christmas I spent with your family?"

"I remember," she whispered against his chest. "We went skiing at Mount Hood." She lifted her head, her eyes brightening slightly at the memory. "You were, as I recall, a terrible skier."

"I'd grown up in Florida," Dan reminded her. "I'd never approached a ski slope before in my life. You've no idea how humiliating it was. I kept thinking of myself as a grown man, but here was this kid—and a girl to boot—skiing circles around me."

Jonnie allowed Dan to pull her down onto his lap in his leather chair. As she recalled the sight of him, cursing a blue streak, flat on his back in the powdery snow, a slight smile curved her lips.

"It wasn't hard to ski circles around you. You spent most of your time in one place."

"You're still a brat." He planted a quick kiss on her soft lips. "Do you remember the second day, when Jason dared me to go up on the fall line?"

"I remember. Dad was furious at him when he found out. He said you could've broken your leg and wiped out an entire career."

Dan chuckled, a deep comforting sound Jonnie could feel against her. "When I got up there and looked at that slope, knowing the only way back down was on those damnable skis, I was never so scared in my life. You were the only thing that kept me from crawling down on my hands and knees.''

''Me? I wasn't even there.''

''No, but I kept thinking about you, flashing down those slopes, your long hair flying behind you like some scarlet banner of courage. You appeared absolutely lion-hearted and I knew I couldn't be upstaged by a cute kid. If you could do it, then so could I.''

''That's silly. Dad had me on skis by the time I was three years old. You were a novice, Dan. No one expected you to be perfect.''

''I wanted to be. At everything.''

Engrossed by the intense expression on his face, Jonnie forgot her fear about his upcoming trip. ''And now?'' she asked softly. ''Do you still want to be perfect, Dan?''

''I try, babe. God help me, I try.''

Jonnie had the vague feeling Dan was telling her something that went far beyond the subject of a long-ago skiing trip. She reached up, her palm pressing against his cheek.

''You're a good man, Dan Kincade. And I'm going to miss you while you're gone.''

''Five days, Jonnie. You can spend those thinking about our reunion celebration.''

Five days. In five days her work here should be finished and she'd be gone. But she didn't know quite how to bring that up right now. He'd seemed disinclined to spend any time yesterday discussing her investigation after her promise that she hadn't planted the story in the press. Did that mean he believed her? Or that he'd accepted her role on the commission and was easily satisfied with a brief relationship consisting of casual sex until her work here was completed?

This relationship was so difficult. Jonnie felt as if she were working her way across her minefield without a map. Dan was impossible. He only allowed fleeting glimpses of the man inside the carefully constructed image, and she felt even those were accidental. On top of that, she was acting so uncharacteristically she could hardly recognize herself. Jonnie had always been like the rest of her clan, open and honest about her feelings. The Ryans placed their cards on the table and let the chips fall where they may. But she was being as secretive as Dan. The two of them were shadow dancing in circles, getting nowhere fast.

"Five days," she murmured, surrendering her worrisome thoughts for a long, passionate kiss. "Be careful, Dan."

"I will. And don't worry, Ryan. I'll be back before you know I'm gone."

I doubt that, she thought as she watched him walk down the long corridor, his head tilted as he listened to the assistant coach at his side. *Because I miss you already, Dan. And I'm so confused I don't know what to do.*

Jonnie made the decision that, as soon as she finished up the investigation at the College of the Cascades, she'd take a long weekend and go down to Mt. Shasta and visit her father. He knew Dan better than anyone. Perhaps he could explain the enigma of the man she loved.

Jonnie spent the next five days going over travel vouchers, recruiting records and expense reimbursements to Dan and his two assistant coaches. And thinking about Dan Kincade. The hours had seemed like months, the days like years, but he was finally coming home tonight.

She felt as if she might be getting a cold, but steadfastly refused to slacken her work pace. Winter colds were part and parcel of living in the Pacific Northwest; it was something she'd learned to live with, like the mold she was continually scrubbing off her bathroom tile.

Despite Jonnie's plans for a leisurely bath before Dan's arrival, her work kept her at the college longer than planned. She'd just arrived back at her hotel room when he knocked on her door.

"You're ruining my work." Dan didn't mince words as Jonnie opened the door to him.

She dropped a quick curtsy. "Why, thank you, Coach Kincade. I see absence *does* make the heart grow fonder, after all."

Dan's mouth melded with hers as a hand moved to the back of her head, holding her to a long, leisurely kiss.

"What do you want me to say," he murmured, his lips resting against her temple, "that you drive me crazy? That you make me so distracted I can't think straight? That I'm finding it impossible to get you out of my mind, even during a road trip as important as the one we just finished up?" His blue eyes were filled with desperation as he stared into her own love-softened ones.

"It's the same for me, Dan. It's like I'm looking at life through a camera lens with a short depth of field. Everything else just blurs in the background. All I want is to make love to you. To feel you holding me, moving inside me again."

His tongue slid deliciously into the depths of her mouth as his hands burned blazing trails down her back, over the soft swell of her hips. His fingers inched their way up her legs under her heavy wool skirt, his moan of gratification echoing her own. Jonnie felt the hardening of his body as he massaged her nylon-clad thighs, and she leaned into his embrace.

Then, she felt a loss as Dan suddenly retrieved his hand and straightened her disheveled clothing.

"Lord, Jonnie, you're complicating my life."

Their gazes held in that little pool of silence, and Jonnie watched the mask slide back down over Dan's features, effectively hiding his despair.

"I certainly don't mean to complicate your life, Dan. I just want—"

"I know what you want, Jonnie," he cut in, almost harshly, "but I'm not certain you realize what you really want. I think you're doing your best to be a modern, liberated lady. One who knows where she's going and is going to let nothing stand in her way. But, deep down, you're still Tom Ryan's little girl who thinks the ideal life revolves around love, laughter, and a houseful of noisy kids. And to tell you the truth, that side of you scares me more than the first."

Jonnie knew she was venturing into dangerous territory with her question, but she asked it anyway. "Dan, if it wasn't for the commission, would you feel the same way about our relationship? Would you still consider it all wrong?"

"Yes."

"Why?"

"I told you, Jonnie," Dan returned swiftly, automatically. "Part of me still feels guilty about this entire affair. I keep expecting Tom to break down the door and beat the hell out of me for daring to compromise his daughter."

"I wish you'd spend a little less time worrying about Dad's feelings and more thinking of mine, Dan."

He sighed. "I know, babe, I know. And I'm doing my damnedest to put it into perspective. Just try to be patient, okay?"

His deep velvet tone melted away her flash of irritation, and Jonnie nodded.

"How about dinner?" he asked after a long pause. "Have you eaten?" His judicious appraisal focused on her nose. "You look like Rudolph. Are you getting a cold?"

"You *are* complimentary tonight, Dan Kincade," Jonnie muttered, wondering what had happened to the romantic reunion she'd envisioned.

She'd pictured a crackling fire, a bottle of champagne, lying in his arms while they whispered words of love. She'd even bought a ridiculously expensive negligee. The soft sea-green complemented her creamy skin tone, her eyes and her coppery hair, and it could have been woven of cobwebs, the material was so sheer. It had been a wonderful fantasy.

But here she was, still dressed in the skirt and sweater she'd worn while working, and all he could do was tell her how unattractive she looked.

"That's not it at all." His tone was immediately conciliatory. "I was just worrying about you."

Well, that was something, she acknowledged. *You didn't worry about someone you didn't care about, did you?*

"I'll get my coat," she decided instantly.

Dan stopped her with his hands on her shoulders. "It's pouring out there. It might be better if we ate in."

Jonnie agreed wholeheartedly. She certainly wasn't eager to venture out in that storm. But she wasn't about to turn down a chance to be with Dan, either.

"Downstairs in the dining room, then?"

"We could do that. Or we could order room service."

I love you, Dan Kincade, she thought. *And I hate this trouble between us. I can't continue to live this way.*

"Can we discuss the commission?"

"I'll try," Dan answered slowly. "But I don't promise that it'll be the easiest conversation we've ever had, Jonnie."

"I know," she replied solemnly. "And thank you. I would like to stay in, Dan. In fact, if you don't mind, I think I'll slip into something a little more comfortable."

It was a cliché, but Jonnie was determined to make the most of this evening. Her eyes promised the reunion she'd been planning these long, lonely days.

"That's a good idea," he agreed instantly, reading the message in her loving gaze. "I'll order dinner."

Her hair curled from the steam in the bathroom, a fluffy auburn cloud drifting over the shoulders of her floor-length emerald silk robe. Not wanting to take a chance on sneezing at an inopportune moment, she swallowed a cold capsule. Then, on further consideration, she took a second.

The room-service waiter was leaving as Jonnie emerged from the bathroom. She lifted the stainless-steel covers, not surprised to discover Dan had ordered his usual steak, this time smothered in mushrooms. Did the man ever eat anything but red meat?

Tentatively she raised the cover on her own meal and found a bowl of steaming, enticingly fragrant soup.

"Vegetarian vegetable," he answered her inquiring glance. "Nothing to make you fall off the alfalfa wagon."

"I don't remember seeing that on the menu."

"It isn't. The chef made it up specially when I explained I had this gorgeous woman up here who looked as if she might be coming down with a cold and refused to eat anything that was good for her."

"Good for me?" Jonnie pointed at his plate with her spoon. "I'll have you know, Daniel Kincade, my diet is far healthier than all that cholesterol and fat you're constantly putting away."

"Then why are you the one with the red nose?" Dan grinned, taking a long swallow of the draft beer he'd ordered to accompany the thick steak.

They ate in comfortable silence but Jonnie knew they were both avoiding what they'd promised to discuss—the commission. The subject hovered over them, a small threatening black cloud. Jonnie was pulled both ways. Part of her wanted to talk about it openly, dispelling Dan's apparent lingering doubts. But another part of her only wanted to savor this moment without introducing harsh reality.

Was Dan right? Was she trying for too much? Was it impossible to want a career and a loving family? In hoping for both was she only opening herself up to disappointment? To failure? If she ever obtained both, would she only do a halfway job in each area, not succeeding at either?

She shook her head, refusing to consider this for the moment. The hearty vegetable soup was delicious, and she discovered the wine Dan had ordered to accompany it effectively numbed the slight headache she'd had all day.

"If you'd gotten a suite, this next move would be a lot easier."

Jonnie looked up as Dan returned from placing the portable table outside in the hallway. Lost in thought, she'd not even noticed his leaving. She was suddenly floating on air. The wine, combined with the cold capsules, had conspired to make her woozy, and she struggled to focus on his face.

"A suite? Do you have any idea what would happen if the taxpayers discovered the Murdock Commission's investigator was putting hotel suites on her expense account? It's probably bad enough I'm not commuting."

"I could always pay."

"What of your reputation around here, Coach Kincade? I thought you were Eugene's Mr. Clean?"

He grimaced. "You make me sound like some type of bathroom cleanser. Obviously I need to update my image. I've always thought keeping a woman labeled you as a man of the world."

Jonnie lifted a finger, wagging it at him. Her eyes attempted to focus on her peach-tipped nail. Was it one finger or two?

"If you paid my expenses," she warned, "I'd have to make a full report, disclosing everything."

"You would, would you?"

She nodded gravely. "I would indeed."

"And what if I explained to the commission that I'd only gotten the suite so we could discuss business? Without compromising the lady investigator by moving to the only comfortable piece of furniture in this room?"

"It certainly wouldn't be the first time."

Jonnie chuckled on a throaty note, weaving to the foot of the bed. Dan grabbed the glass of wine from her hand just in time as she fell face forward onto the queen-sized mattress.

"I think you're smashed, counselor." The deep voice was heavily laced with indulgent amusement.

Jonnie rolled over onto her back, held out her arms and smiled a soft, inviting smile.

"On two glasses of wine? Don't be ridiculous, Coach. It's probably just the cold pills." Her glazed eyes sparkled up at him. "You're not afraid of catching anything, are you?"

Dan gave her his answer as he deliberately placed the glass on the dresser, kicked off his shoes and joined her on the bed. His elbow sank into the pillow as he lay on his side, his head braced on his palms. He didn't return Jonnie's smile, observing her gravely instead.

"No matter how much I know this is wrong for both of us, I can't keep away from you," he admitted softly, his deep voice roughened velvet. "You drive everything else from my mind. Do you realize that?"

Jonnie tried to focus on the somber, handsome face just inches from her own. She reached up and ran her palm along his jawline. Jonnie loved the feel and woody scent of him when he'd recently shaved. But she was also not at all averse to the pleasant pain his late-afternoon beard could inflict as it grazed her skin. She moved her fingers downward, exploring the deep cleft in his chin before tracing the outline of his lips.

When she slid a finger to the center of his parted lips, Dan sucked it hungrily, causing a surge of warmth deep in her thighs. Jonnie could tell Dan wanted her every bit as much as she wanted him right now. For he was right; despite their problems, they were drawn to each other with uncommon strength.

His hand moved over her body, causing her blood to turn even hotter as he untied the belt of her silk robe. She'd dressed with this end in mind, and as the emerald material was folded back, Dan's eyes feasted on the enticing expanse of skin revealed by the cut of the filmy nightgown.

"Beautiful," he said with a deep sigh. "Ivory satin." His dark head lowered as his lips sought to explore the newly exposed skin. "Did you buy this just for me?" he asked, loving the idea.

When Jonnie failed to answer, Dan levered himself up, gazing in curiosity at her face. Her tawny gold lashes rested against her cheeks, and soft puffs of breath escaped her slightly parted lips as she slept.

Dan slid her under the sheets, gave her one very long last look, and let himself out of her room.

Chapter Nine

"How do you feel?" Dan stood in the doorway of Jonnie's temporary campus office eyeing her wading her way through the stacks of files.

"Terrible." Her expression was gloomy as she gazed out from heavy-lidded eyes. A tiny tracery of red lines ran in delicate patterns across her bleary whites, like scarlet lace. "I feel exactly as if I had a hang-over...on two damn glasses of wine." She rubbed her temples with her fingertips. "When did you leave?"

"Right after you passed out from mixing cold pills and wine. Wine I never would've given you if I'd known about the pills before dinner. Not too bright a move, counselor."

"I wasn't thinking," she answered absently, trying to focus her thoughts on another matter nagging at her mind. "Did we ever talk about my work?"

"No."

She could tell by the shortly issued monosyllable that Dan wasn't inclined to talk this morning, either. How long could they go on this way? They were working hard to pretend her commission away. They were not allowed to discuss love, or trust, or any emotion other than a simple sexual need. This entire relationship was built on a tissue of deceptions. It could never withstand the test of time.

"Dan, about that—"

"Did you see this morning's paper?" he interrupted.

Jonnie shook her head, wishing she hadn't as the rocks inside began tumbling about.

"Perhaps you should." Dan handed it to her, moving aside a stack of manila folders to sit on the corner of her desk. He was silent as she read the latest in a series of "leaks" still hinting at misdeeds at the College of Cascades.

When she'd finished reading the carefully written articles, she braced her elbows on the desk top, covering her face for a long time. When she lifted her head, her eyes pleaded for understanding.

"I had nothing to do with this . . . I can't let you see my preliminary report, so you'll have to trust me. But there's nothing in it that remotely resembles these accusations."

"I know." His mouth quirked slightly in a grim little smile as he took both her hands in his. Jonnie could feel her blood responding as his thumb made little paths on the tender skin of her palm.

"You believe me?"

"I do. I gave it a lot of thought while I was away and came to the conclusion you really didn't know what was going on. And I apologize for ever thinking differently. I should've known Tom Ryan's daughter wouldn't use tactics like that. She'd be a straight shooter, all the way."

"It was understandable for you to resent me," Jonnie admitted readily. "William *is* trying to use the commission to further his own political career. You saw it coming, but I was too caught up in the zealous role of Jonnie Ryan, Girl Reformer."

Dan brought her hands to his lips, and his eyes were warm as they observed her flushed face.

"You may be a hotshot attorney, Ryan, but you're a babe in the woods when it comes to bare-knuckles fighting." He smiled, his expression more unguarded than she'd ever seen it. "Now that you're resigning from the commission, we won't have any more problems on that score."

Jonnie's eyes flew open. "Resign? Dan, I'm not going to resign. Where did you get that idea?"

A puzzled frown furrowed his forehead, and his ebony brows lowered toward his broken nose. He looked incredibly formidable right now, and Jonnie wished she were somewhere, anywhere else.

As Dan glared down at her, he wished he could fully understand Jonnie Ryan. On the one hand, she was the most loving woman he'd ever known. He could care about her deeply, he'd realized during those days of separation while he'd been on the road. But her ambition made him increasingly uneasy. If the day came when Jonnie was forced to choose between her career and him—and he knew it would—what in hell would she do?

His answering tone was tight and his words were edged razor sharp. "I assumed once you realized the snake pit you were working in, you'd want to leave. Perhaps I overestimated what we've got going for us."

He dropped her hands abruptly, and Jonnie felt a surge of irritation. He'd never promised her any permanency, never told her that he loved her—something she'd give everything she possessed to hear. How dare he try to get her to stop her work?

"Perhaps you did, Dan. After all, you're the one who set the ground rules. I believe you wanted an affair. A short affair with no ties, so I could prove I was adult enough to handle it—like the rest of your women."

"You've got a good memory, Jonnie." He slid off the desk and left the office in long, angry strides.

Jonnie didn't know whether to be relieved or distressed when she didn't see him for the rest of the day. She tried her best to focus on the rows of figures, but she might as well have been attempting to read Sanskrit. Dan's features appeared embossed on every sheet of paper she studied.

"I'm sorry." She looked up to see him filling the doorway, his expression conciliatory. "I've no business telling you what to do. Especially since you've got me dead to rights. I'm the one who set those dumb rules for our relationship. And I'm the one who's been backing away because of my feelings for that cute, stubborn, red-haired spitfire I once knew."

His words caused a spark of hope to stir the cold ashes he'd made of her heart. She moved toward him meeting him halfway, in the center of the small room.

Dan's long fingers curved about her upper arms. "You're the most ambitious and fascinating woman I've ever known, Jonnie Ryan. You make my blood boil, whether I want to ravish you or turn you over my knee. I don't know how long we're going to be able to continue this way, with your damn commission continually interfering."

"It won't, Dan."

He tilted his head back, looking down at her, and Jonnie knew he was struggling to keep the gleam of hope from brightening his deep blue eyes.

"What do you mean by that?"

"I mean that I'm all finished. I'm writing my final report tomorrow and turning it in. Whatever problems you have with our relationship from now on, Dan, you're not going to be able to blame on the Murdock Commission."

His gaze moved over her face, probing into her eyes, searching for something.

"Am I allowed to inquire as to the nature of this report?"

"You can ask, but I can't tell you." His fingers bore down on the soft skin of her arms, and she felt his tension. "Don't worry, Dan. There's not a negative thing on it, except the fact that two of your players have been issued eight away uniforms this season. Which is not exactly cost-efficient, but not enough to hang you, either." She smiled.

"Bradshaw and Grimes. The two biggest slobs on the team. They used to leave them under beds, on locker-room floors. Once they left their bags in the Houston airport. We solved that problem, though."

"I noticed the losses seemed to stop in early December," Jonnie agreed, demonstrating an eye for detail that unnerved Dan.

"That's because we shuffled the room assignments around. Now they each bunk with the team neatniks. It's like giving them den mothers."

She laughed. "I knew you were a brilliant strategist."

"You're not so bad yourself, Ryan. Even with that cute little red nose." He dropped a light kiss on the tip. "At least after your little drunk last night your eyes match it."

Jonnie allowed him to help her into her coat. When she turned to look up at him, his eyes held more of a spark of mischief than they had all week. Her gaze drank in the softened features of this man she loved, moving from the top of his jet black head down his hard, masculine frame.

"You'd better be careful, Kincade," she teased, putting her fingertips to her lips and pressing them against his. "If you keep handing out those chivalrous, flowery compliments, a girl might get the idea you care about her or something."

She gave him a breathtaking smile as she picked up her umbrella and left the office, blowing him a kiss.

William Murdock read Jonnie's finalized report in silence, his expression giving nothing away. Finally, he leaned back in his chair and lit a cigarette, drawing in a long, deep breath before expelling a spiral of gray smoke.

"You've worked in politics long enough to understand the importance of political maneuvering in the most innocent of activities, Jonnie."

"I do," she agreed slowly. "I haven't always liked the idea, but..."

"But, we can't do anyone a bit of good unless we get elected," he pointed out. "Sometimes, so long as you don't break any laws, the end does justify the means."

Jonnie nodded, waiting for him to expound on the theory she'd heard often enough before.

"I've got big plans. For my career and for the state," he continued. "I've every intention of becoming the next attorney general and this commission will pave the way. But only if we do it right."

William stabbed the cigarette in her direction, apparently deciding it was time to remove the kid gloves.

"I tried to warn you, Ryan, that if I saw any more of this fan-club stuff, I'd replace you with someone more skilled in this type of assignment."

Witch-hunt, she corrected mentally, feeling a black cloud of dread settle over her. Dan had been right all along. William had never intended to allow her to find everything shipshape in the Cascade's athletic department. He was going to climb right over Dan in order to win the party's nomination, then the election. And what was galling was the fact that he expected her to help him construct the damn ladder.

For a fleeting moment, Jonnie considered handing in her resignation and returning to Dan, her head held high, telling him proudly what she'd done. It would be a sacrifice, but she'd do anything for Dan Kincade, the man she loved.

A warning gong of common sense tolled in her mind. If she were to withdraw, William would only replace her with someone who'd aim directly for the jugular. While the records had been squeaky clean so far, Jonnie knew how figures could be twisted to suit anyone's purpose. What was the old adage? Figures lie while liars figure.

"All right, William," she said quietly. "I'll try to do better." She rose from the chair, moving toward the door, her calm exterior not betraying for a moment her inner anguish.

"Ryan?"

She turned, eyeing him over her shoulder. "Yes?"

"Don't bother. I expect everyone to pull his weight around here, and you've let the team down. So you're benched for the rest of the season."

All color left her face. "You're taking me off the commission?"

"Let's just say you're taking a leave of absence," he suggested smoothly, "for your health. You do look as if you're coming down with a cold, by the way."

"Thank you, William. You're a real pal," Jonnie muttered, receiving a small measure of pleasure as she slammed the door with all her might.

Chapter Ten

Jonnie's head rested against the back of the high seat, her eyes squeezed shut and her stomach doing somersaults as she waited for the takeoff. Her head ached, and her nose was running. But it was more than that. An instinctive, deep-seated fear of flying was smothering her in its black mist. Her nostrils were filled with the acrid scent of smoke, but Jonnie didn't bother opening her eyes to see what was burning. Because she knew nothing was. Not now. It was merely a sensory flashback to that long-ago crash.

Her fingers gripped the arms of her seat as the cries in her head reached a fevered pitch, overcoming the whining of the huge jetliner's engines.

It'll be all right, she told herself. *It's safer than driving a car. Safer than taking a bath. This plane won't crash. It wouldn't dare crash. It's got to take me to Denver...and Dan.*

Jonnie refused the snack offered by the flight attendant and spent the flight locked in her own world of private horrors, only returning to reality when the plane had set down on the Denver runway and she was wrapped safely in the arms of a surprised but pleased Dan Kincade.

"I can't believe you got on that thing to come to me," he said, looking over her shoulder at the plane.

"It's too bad we've got to get to the stadium or I'd reward you for bravery above and beyond the call of duty." His eyes, as they returned to her face, were teasingly suggestive.

"I'm not on the commission any longer, Dan," Jonnie blurted out, watching his face for his reaction.

It moved in waves across his strong features—first surprise, then suspicion, then acceptance. Then a relief she couldn't comprehend. She knew they still had a problem. The commission had only been the tip of the iceberg in Dan's refusal to allow a deep and lasting relationship. So why was he looking as if he'd just been handed his Christmas presents eleven months early?

"We'll talk about it later," he said, walking her to the door where he had a taxi waiting to take them to the stadium.

The game was an unmitigated disaster from the opening jump ball. The players in the starting lineup for the Denver Mustangs seemed to be taller than telephone booths. And three of the players were definitely going to make the franchise wherever they ended up in the pros. Richardson, the Cascade player who lived by blocking shots, was given a rough lesson in one-upmanship by a power player on the Mustangs who blocked a total of twenty shots and scared away dozens more. The young player was even bigger than his teammates, resembling a Coke machine with a head.

One Denver player seemed more Pegasus than Mustang, defying the laws of gravity as he flew through the air, blithely dropping the ball into the basket whenever he pleased.

"I'm going to that kid's graduation and cheer my head off," Dan muttered, flinging himself into a chair in front of Jonnie.

"He's good," she murmured.

"Damn good," he agreed, not taking his eyes from the game, "but he's getting a lot of help. Our guys know all the scouts are here and they're showing off their damn dribbling talents. It's as if they've never heard of the pass."

At the sharp retort of the referee's whistle, Dan was on his feet, loudly protesting yet another foul on one of his players. His actions were intense and furious, yet controlled, as he stopped just short of earning a technical foul himself.

"Trouble with officials is, they don't care who wins," he growled, throwing his tall body onto the metal folding chair with a harsh, powerful motion.

Jonnie had been around the sport long enough to know not to answer. A few seconds later the buzzer mercifully sounded, ending the half, the College of the Cascade's Lumberjacks trailing 47-25.

Whatever Dan told them during half time seemed to have some effect. Playing as if they expected every shot to fail, the Lumberjacks positioned themselves under the basket for the rebounds, effectively utilizing their fast break.

Just when it appeared the team might stage a come-from-behind victory, the Mustang skywalker was back, facing the determined Richardson once again. The tall, lanky forward faked his head left, then right, then suddenly pushed the ball between the slower guard's legs, grabbed it and proceeded to dunk it, earning a wild burst of appreciation from the hometown crowd filling the Mustang's stadium.

It was as if the stunning play had punctured a balloon. All the air seemed to leave the Lumberjacks, and after an agonizingly long final quarter, they were allowed to escape, the final score 102-68.

Jonnie lingered in the hallway outside the locker room, cringing as she heard the sounds that were a portent of how this season would go until the team managed to put their act together and play as they'd been coached. Basketball coaches were not known for their laid-back attitude, and Dan was no exception as the slamming of locker doors was punctuated by a harsh inquiry.

"Have any of you guys seen Johnson's jump shot? What the hell happened, Johnson," the heavily sarcastic tone sliced through the still air, "did you leave it on the plane?"

The responding mumblings were low, and Jonnie wished she could find someplace to hide before Dan emerged. She didn't want any of that fury directed toward her. Perhaps this had been a bad idea all along, she considered bleakly.

But, when he finally joined her, Dan managed a weak grin. "Now I know how Napoleon felt." His voice was strained from shouting throughout the game and wasn't much more than a husky whisper as he put his arm around her and led her out of the deserted building. "They ought to rename this place Waterloo Arena."

The wind blew the snow sideways, stinging Jonnie's cheeks as they walked toward the chartered bus. Dan pulled her against him, holding her face to the thick sheepskin collar of his overcoat.

"God, it's cold," she moaned. Despite the deep, drifted snow, her long stride managed to keep up with his.

"You should have stayed in Salem," he scolded as the driver opened the door of the bus for them. The engine was idling, and it was warm inside.

"I had to be with you," she said, wanting to explain. She wanted to have everything out in the open, once and for all—William Murdock, the Murdock Commission, and her love.

"I can't say that I'm unhappy to have you here, Jonnie," he interrupted to reassure her, his blue eyes warmer than the hot breeze blasting from the bus heater. "But we're not going to have any time alone until we get back to Oregon. You would've been better off avoiding this Rocky Mountain weather and staying home in bed—waiting for me."

He smiled with a friendly leer, and Jonnie thought for a moment he might kiss her, but the sound of male voices coming toward the bus through the swirl of snow precluded it.

The snow swirled against the windows of the bus, and the driver took the icy roads slowly, the yellow headlights barely cutting through the dark and wind-blown sleet. Dan was sitting with the assistant coaches, and every once in a while Jonnie would see him look back at her, his eyes darkening with a vaguely speculative expression. It was impossible to divine what he was thinking, and soon Jonnie gave up trying altogether as her mind became obsessed with a problem far more overwhelming.

She couldn't do it. She just couldn't, she determined as the bus finally pulled up outside the airline terminal. It was bad enough flying in the daytime, in good weather, when her mind could rationally accept that the terrors were in her own subconscious.

But this—squalls of icy sleet buffeted by fierce gusts, snow building up on every horizontal surface—was too much. Her high-heeled boots slipped on the icy sidewalk, and she fell forward, steadied just in time by a pair of strong hands. Hands she'd know anywhere.

Jonnie's eyes were wide with terror. "Dan, I can't."

"I don't think you'll have to," he said. "It looks as if our rotten luck's going to continue. No one's flying out of here tonight."

From his grim, accepting tone, Jonnie knew she should be sympathizing with him. But she couldn't. She felt as if she'd just been given a last-minute reprieve from the governor on her way to the electric chair.

Dan's laugh was deep and husky as he watched the relief wash over her face in waves. "And since you're so damn sexy," he rasped in her ear, "I'll even forgive you for not realizing this is lousy news for me."

Instantly her relief gave way to contrition. "Oh, Dan. I'm sorry."

"That's okay, Ryan," he assured her, putting his arm around her waist to keep her from slipping on the icy concrete as they made their way to the glass doors of the terminal. "Just remember what you're going to be missing. I'd hoped to get home in plenty of time to make an early bed check."

The throaty, husky tone was definitely provocative and Jonnie no longer felt the cold as she realized they'd managed to truly put the commission aside. Now all she had to do was determine what made him so unwilling to face his own needs and feelings. Then everything would be perfect.

The Denver weather was doing nothing to help her shake her cold, and Jonnie hunched her shoulders, wrapping her arms about herself. All flights had been canceled, and she had no idea how many people were stranded. Dan left her for a time, returning to direct her to a molded plastic chair he'd located, which wasn't already claimed. Her head throbbed, and she felt as if she had a fever. A fit of coughing overtook her, waking the baby who'd been sleeping peacefully in the arms of a young woman seated next to her.

At the infant's squalls, Jonnie apologized. "I'm sorry."

The mother only glared in response, making Jonnie hunker down even further into the hard chair.

"Here." At the wonderfully familiar deep voice, Jonnie looked up to see Dan standing over her, holding out a Styrofoam cup. A mist of steam rose from it and she cradled it in her hands, smiling gratefully.

"Tea. Thank you."

He shrugged. "Tea was easy. Now we've got to figure out what else to do with you." His eyes narrowed as he studied her critically. Squatting down, he placed the back of his hand against her forehead.

"Damn it, Jonnie Ryan, you've got one helluva fever. You should be home in bed."

At his gritty outburst, the young woman gathered her baby to her breast and scurried off, obviously not caring to chance anything contagious.

"Now look what you did," Jonnie complained. "That poor lady is going to have to carry that baby around all night. There aren't any vacant chairs."

"Someone will give her one," he answered, folding his tall frame into the abandoned seat. "Don't worry about her. Try worrying about yourself for a change."

"It's just my usual winter cold," Jonnie snuffled, feeling her ears pop as she blew her nose.

"I think it's a lot more than that. But whatever you've got, Jonnie, you belong in bed."

A sparkle lit Jonnie's watery eyes, despite her misery. "Now that's the best idea you've come up with all night. But aren't you afraid you'll catch something?"

"You know you're asking for it." Dan's eyes were a warm caress as they moved over her flushed face. "Right here. In front of everyone, and you wouldn't be able to do a thing to stop me."

"Boy, what an over-inflated ego," she protested, her smile wobbly as a dull ache persisted behind her eyes. "I'd never be that far gone, Dan Kincade."

"Want to bet?" His voice was a silky threat as he covered her knee with his palm, the simple touch sending sparks spiraling through her leg and up her spine.

"All right," she acquiesced weakly. "Let's just give you the benefit of the doubt and not put it to the test."

"Coward."

His voice was vibrant with passion, and Jonnie knew that if she were to die from this cold right now, at least she'd have experienced heaven in Dan's arms before going.

She was about to attempt a clever comeback when another series of deep coughs wracked her body, draining her of any energy.

"Damn. You are really sick, babe."

Dan took off his coat and wrapped her in it, taking the empty cup from her fingers. Brushing his fingertips along her cheek, he pulled her against his shoulder.

"Try to sleep, Jonnie."

"I'll try. And, Dan...?"

"What?"

"Thank you for being so good to me."

A muscle jerked in his cheek, but his only answer was given by his hand as it brushed down her hair. Jonnie relaxed in the warm cradle of his arms, her fingers massaging against his shirt front like a kitten settling down for the night.

They remained quiet for a long time, and Jonnie finally lifted her eyes to his face, wondering if he was even awake. Her gaze collided with somber blue ones. "Dan?"

"Ummm?"

"I can't sleep."

Dan's roving gaze took in the crowded terminal, stranded travelers now giving up and spreading out on whatever flat surface was available. There were bodies sprawled over counters, chairs and the floor. Children cried or complained bitterly in high, strident whines. Travelers who were able to sleep were snoring away, apparently as comfortable in whatever makeshift accommodations they'd settled upon as they were in their own beds. Others were reading, unable or unwilling to surrender to the indignity of sleeping with total strangers.

The travelers had been here for hours, and from the looks of the storm raging outside the plate glass windows they'd be here a lot longer. Jonnie's eyes were glazed and feverish. Bright, unnatural spots were like scarlet flags waving in her cheeks.

"Jonnie, I'll be right back. Okay, honey?" Dan brushed her damp hair from her face with gentle fingers, sliding deftly from her tight embrace.

Jonnie tried to focus on him, her heart only noting that he'd called her honey. It was the first endearment, other than the casual "babe," she'd heard from those full lips. *He's starting to love me,* she thought, hugging the idea to herself. *He's really beginning to admit he loves me. I knew he would.*

"Come on, babe."

"Dan? Where are we going?"

Jonnie's confused glance moved to the windows, seeing only the whirling whiteness highlighted by the outdoor floodlights.

"Oh no. Is the plane taking off?"

There was an edge of hysteria in her voice, which Dan hastened to dispel. "No, honey. Nothing's taking off yet. I just want to show you something."

She allowed him to lead her through the throng of people, her hand lost in his. As they reached a doorway marked Flight Service Crews Only Jonnie tugged on her hand.

"Dan, we're not allowed in here."

"Hush, woman, you're only going to draw a crowd." He gave her a quick kiss, then a devilish wink of one blue eye before continuing through the heavy red metal door.

The gust of wind blew a swirl of sleet into her face, and Jonnie gasped from the shock of the cold as well as the tall apparition making its way through the dark toward them. The creature was huge, with enormous hands and a face whose complexion was mottled shades of yellow and green. She wondered vaguely if she was sicker than she thought and was now delirious.

"All gassed up and ready to go, Dan." The apparition had a voice, and as he lumbered toward them through the snow, Jonnie realized belatedly it was nothing more than a very large man wearing a ski mask. She giggled, feeling incredibly foolish and more lightheaded than ever.

"I thought he was the abominable snowman," she gasped over laughter which couldn't seem to be suppressed.

Dan didn't share her laughter. Instead, his blue eyes narrowed at her almost hysterical amusement at such a simple misconception. He didn't like the way she looked. Perhaps once he got her settled, he ought to call a doctor.

Jonnie's bubbling laughter ceased as rapidly as it had begun, as if she were a clock suddenly running down. Dan scooped her into his arms and climbed into the cab of the idling snowcat.

"I appreciate this, Jimmy," he said to the large man who'd begun shifting the gears of the enormous yellow vehicle.

"Hell, Dan, I made a bundle betting on the team when you were in town. It's the least I can do." His eyes slanted away from the sleet-covered windshield for a moment to observe the sleeping woman in Dan's arms. "She doesn't look real good. So that's Jason Ryan's baby sister, huh?"

"That's her."

"Too bad old Tom didn't have five boys. Then he could've had himself his very own team."

"She was a tiger at playground ball," Dan stated abruptly, feeling an odd need to defend Jonnie.

He experienced a sense of pride with the declaration. She had played well for a girl; hell, she'd been better than most of the boys. But it was her bravery that had always earned his attention, her gutsy attitude on and off the court.

"Humph. Doesn't look like she'd be much good right now."

They grew silent, watching the swishing of the wide wipers as they kept the huge snowcat's windshield marginally clear of the building flakes. It was warm inside the cab, but Dan breathed a sigh of relief when the vehicle pulled to a halt in front of a hotel on the outskirts of the Denver Airport property.

"I owe you one, Jimmy." He climbed down from the high cab, bracing the still-sleeping Jonnie against his chest.

"Nah, you don't. Consider it fair reimbursement for what the Mustangs did to your kids tonight."

Dan groaned, suddenly remembering the game. Had it only been this evening the debacle had occurred? How had he forgotten it so soon? Usually after a loss like that he'd still be chewing nails three days later. Jonnie. He glanced down at the sleeping woman nestled in his arms. She'd made the difference. He'd been so busy thinking about her, the game had flown his mind. He didn't remember that ever happening before in all his years as a player or a coach. But then, he admitted, carrying her up to the automatic glass doors, he'd never felt this way about anyone before.

Chapter Eleven

"Dan? What in the world?"

Jonnie stared around the hotel room in confusion as Dan put her down onto the bed. He'd already pushed her coat from her shoulders and had begun to unbutton her cardigan.

Her hands immediately covered his, and her eyes held a real regret. "Oh, Dan. I don't know if I can be very good right now."

Dan laughed gently, his words tinged with regret. "I'm not going to ravish you, honey. As delectable as you may be, I can muster up a reserve of self-control when absolutely necessary. You're sick, Jonnie. And I'm going to take care of you."

Her shoulders slumped as she expelled a weak, grateful sigh. "I'm so glad. I feel awful Dan." Then her eyes widened slightly as she looked around the unmistakable furnishings of a hotel room. "Where are we?"

"I got a room."

"But how? I heard people in the airport talking, and they said every room in town had been taken by stranded travelers."

He chuckled. "Don't forget, honey, while I was playing ball I spent two years in Denver. I can still pull a few favors out of a hat when I need them."

He finished with her sweater, tossing it onto a chair, then unfastened the catch of the lacy bra. Her full breasts spilled forward, and for a long moment Dan had to struggle to remind himself that she was ill. Couldn't he exercise even a modicum of self-restraint around her?

Dan felt the heat rising in him and succumbed just long enough to allow his lips a taste of the delicate rosy crowns gracing her soft, rounded flesh. The soft moan from Jonnie's throat brought his attention sharply back to the matters at hand.

Reluctantly, before he did something he'd regret, Dan unzipped her wool skirt, sliding it over her hips and placing it on the chair with the discarded bra and sweater. Her slip and panty hose were next, and his fingers attempted to be gentle as he peeled them down her fever-heated body.

She was now clad only in brief nylon bikini panties, the dark shadow affecting him almost more than he could bear. He'd never been this way with any other woman. Jonnie Ryan was like a drug that had gotten into his blood, surging through his veins. Dan al-

lowed himself one long, hungry glance at the tantalizing body stretched out on the narrow bed. Then he
expelled a soft sigh, covered her with the sheet and
picked up the telephone, dialing the hotel operator.

"What the hell do you mean there's no doctors
available? What if this was an emergency? What if she
was having a heart attack?"

Dan expelled an exasperated breath in a long angry
hiss as he listened to the patient, drawn-out explanation about closed roads, traffic accidents and standing room only at Denver's hospitals. It appeared
medical care for a woman with a miserable winter cold
was not a top-priority item.

"I'm telling you, it's more than a goddamn cold.
This woman is sick!"

He ground his teeth. "Of course I can't bring her to
the hospital. I had to practically hijack a snowplow
from runway duty to get her into a bed. I'm not going
to take her out in that again."

He listened for a few more minutes, than slammed
the phone down.

"Dan?" Her hand inched across the sheet to where
he sat on the edge of the bed, his hands balled into fists
at his sides.

"Go to sleep, Jonnie, everything's going to be fine."

Her hand caught his as he moved away. "Dan? Will
you stay?"

"Of course I'll stay, Ryan." He managed a light
tone, belying his worry. "Now quit wasting energy on
talking, and get to sleep."

Dan lay down beside her, taking her in his arms. He softened his teasing, murmuring soft comforting words into her ear, his lips seeming scorched by the heat of her dry skin.

Jonnie snuggled against his firm chest. "I love you," she whispered, believing the words remained buried in her mind.

A puzzled frown darkened Dan's face, and his eyes flashed obvious surprise as he looked down at her. The exhaustion brought on by her illness led into sleep, and Jonnie drifted off, missing the studied examination Dan was making of her flushed features.

The storm continued with undiminished energy for hours as Jonnie slept restlessly in Dan Kincade's arms. Her breathing was shallow and strained, and Dan watched her, for the first time in his life feeling totally useless. He'd developed an almost obsessive need to make her better, to take care of her. He hadn't been lying that night he told her she brought out a protective streak in him. At first he'd assumed it was because of their earlier relationship—because he thought of her as that cute kid who'd followed him around like an adoring, affable puppy.

But now there was something far more to his feelings for her. What he was experiencing didn't remotely resemble what he'd felt for that little girl.

Jonnie felt disoriented as she woke and discovered herself wrapped in Dan's strong arms. As her eyes swept the unfamiliar room, she slowly began to recall where she was and why. Dan had stayed with her in the

airport, and he'd located this room. Had he even taken
her for a ride on a snowplow? Was it only a halluci-
nation, or had that huge man with the many-colored
face driven her here? Whatever, Dan had taken care of
her, treating her as if he'd loved her. Well, at least
cared about her.

Slipping carefully from his embrace, she held her
breath as he muttered a few soft words of protest.
Then, after he'd begun to breathe more regularly
again, she tugged the crisp white sheet down to his
waist, allowing herself the pleasure of viewing his
sprawled form. He was lying on his back, and the sight
of his hard, muscled chest brought back memories of
that crisp pelt of ebony hair against her breasts as he'd
wrapped her tightly in his arms while the storm had
raged outside.

Jonnie had never known anyone to sleep so deeply.
She continued to tug the sheet downward, inch by
cautious inch, finally freeing him of the confining
covers.

His toned, athletic body was so beautifully formed!
Her loving gaze moved over his taut hips, down the
pillars of his long legs, and her cheeks went warm with
the memory of how strongly those hair-brushed limbs
had entwined with hers. Returning her gaze slowly to
his face, Jonnie found it surprisingly boyish in re-
pose. It crossed her mind that too often these past
weeks, that ruggedly handsome face had been tightly
set with tension, those beautiful blue eyes shadowed
with caution. Perhaps now that she was no longer on

the commission, he'd stop acting as if she'd been assigned to be his executioner.

How she loved this man! Jonnie couldn't lie next to him another moment without touching him. She reached up, brushing an errant jet curl from his forehead.

"Dan?" she said softly.

Having given up on sorting out their relationship, Dan had finally drifted off to sleep. It took him a moment to remember where they were, but those sea-green eyes, only inches from his own, brought everything crashing back.

His gaze moved over Jonnie's features, finding her color a bit more natural since her sleep. Her hair tumbled, thick and rich, over her shoulders and spilled onto his chest. He vaguely remembered stripping down to his shorts sometime during the night, finding the suit too uncomfortable for sleeping. As he gained awareness, Dan felt her long, satiny legs next to his. As usual, he couldn't fit in the standard hotel bed. This time, however, he didn't mind.

For the first time in his life, he'd slept wonderfully well away from home. Jonnie Ryan fit so well in his arms. Did he dare hope she'd fit as well in his life? Dan realized with a blinding clarity that he loved her. But what chance could they possibly have together? Even if she'd honestly left the commission, the investigation wouldn't stop. Murdock would send another snoop around, and then another and another, until he found his scandal. And then Jonnie Ryan would discover that yet another man she'd made the mistake of trusting had let her down.

This entire relationship was making him feel as if he'd been handed a grenade with the pin already pulled. The question was not *if* the damn thing was going to explode, but *when*.

"How are you feeling?" he asked finally.

"I think I'm better," Jonnie answered. "Thank you for everything, Dan."

"I didn't do that much," he countered. "Not nearly as much as I'd like to have done, anyway."

Jonnie rested her cheek on his chest, filled with a contentment she'd never felt before.

"You should have said something," she murmured, pressing her lips lightly against his skin. She'd become a Dan Kincade junkie—his taste, his touch, his tangy male scent—everything about the man contributed to this dizzying effect on her.

"Good Lord, woman, you were sick! What kind of animal do you take me for?"

Jonnie lifted her gaze to his face, reaching up to trace the full line of his lips with her fingernail. "A magnificently wild one," she determined after a moment's silent deliberation. "With a lot of work, a woman might be able to domesticate you a little, but she'd never tame you."

"Funny," he murmured, "that's exactly how I'd describe you. With a male doing the taming, naturally."

"Naturally." She gave him a soft, feminine smile, then lowered her head, drawing moist circles with her tongue around one tiny nub, glorying in its instant response.

"Minx," he groaned. "Could you at least *try* to remember you're sick?"

"I'm feeling much, much better," she assured him. Her teeth closed around the dark male nipple and tugged, while her hands ran up and down his torso, exploring the broad span of his chest. She trailed her fingers with idle pleasure through the curling hair.

"Jonnie," he warned as she slid her palm along the plane of his flat stomach. "I don't think this is a very good idea."

"Shh..." She pressed her lips lightly against his, silencing his objection. "Why don't you withhold judgment on that for a little while, Dan?" Her fingers trailed the warming flesh of his hips and thighs, finally closing around him.

"My God, woman," he growled softly, "you need a keeper!"

Her sea-green gaze held his for an indefinable time. "I need you," she finally responded, lowering her tawny head.

Dan's self-restraint was threatening to go up in flames at any moment. He thrust his hands into the tousled red-brown cloud of her hair, and before Jonnie's lips could reach their quest, he'd turned her onto her back and pinned her against the mattress. He flung a leg over her thighs, holding her momentarily still.

"I brought you here to take care of you, Jonnie Ryan. And by God, that's precisely what I'm going to do."

At the intensity of his husky voice, Jonnie's eyes misted with the realization of how much Dan did care for her, but her smile still reached him.

"I've got a few suggestions along that line," she tempted prettily.

Dan rolled to his side, propping himself up on one elbow. With the fingers of his free hand, he brushed a few strands of fiery, sleep-tousled hair from her face.

"There's nothing I'd rather do than stay in bed with you all day, sweetheart." He sighed, shaking his head with mute frustration. His fingers trailed down her cheek and along her throat, where he felt her pulse beating a wild rhythm. Her eyes grew liquid with desire as he caressed the slope of her breast, and Dan knew he was only prolonging both their agony. Because, despite the fact that she honestly did appear a little better after a night's sleep, he knew Jonnie was far from well.

"I want you to stay here in bed," Dan announced as he reluctantly left the bed. "I'll go down and see what I can find to eat."

"All right," Jonnie acquiesced with uncharacteristic meekness, knowing he only had her welfare in mind. But she wished that just this once, he'd been a bit less concerned about her health.

After he left on his search for breakfast, she made it to the bathroom, groaning as she viewed her image in the mirror. She combed her fingers through her sleep-tousled hair, trying to tame the tumbling waves. She'd felt her fever break sometime during her restless sleep, and now strands of hair were clinging to her forehead. How was she ever going to impress him enough to make him realize how perfect she was for him?

In her desire to make herself more attractive, Jonnie threw good sense to the wind and took a shower, the effort more exhausting than she'd imagined. She managed to wrap a towel around her and sank into the chair at the desk as dizziness overcame her. Dan had taken the contents out of his suit pockets the night before, and as her wet hands gripped the corner of the small desk, drops of moisture fell onto some papers he'd left on the cluttered surface.

"Damn."

She began blotting at them vigorously, hoping to dry the papers before the ink smeared. There was his ticket. And a stub from his pass to the arena last night. God, the game! She'd forgotten that disaster. No wonder he'd been out of sorts this morning. Her father had been known not to exorcise the demons of a loss like that for several days afterward.

As she rubbed at his checkbook with the corner of her towel, Jonnie couldn't help noticing some of the entries. He spent too much time eating out, she mused, taking in all the stubs made out to restaurants. That couldn't be good for him. Especially if he lived only on a diet of red meat and black coffee she'd witnessed so far. When they were married, she'd take care of him.

Jonnie knew Dan would never agree to becoming a vegetarian, even with her modified diet allowing dairy products and eggs. Yet, if handled gently, he could probably be eased toward better habits. A little poultry and fish, cooked in appealing ways, could add twenty years to his life. To their life together.

So lost was she in her pleasant domestic fantasy that Jonnie missed, at first, the significance of the name that occurred several times in the list of expenditures. Then, like a bolt from the blue, it hit, bursting her bubble of contentment.

"You got out of bed."

Jonnie spun in the direction of his voice, blanching to a pale pewter as she viewed Dan standing in the doorway, a white bakery bag and a carton carrying two cups of coffee in his hands. His steely blue gaze was directed to the checkbook she still held in her hand.

Dan's cold, accusing eyes raked over her, seeming to strip the white terry towel from her body, before returning to her trembling hands and the damning checkbook.

"When I accused you of doing anything to ruin me and Cascades, I spoke out of frustration. But now I see I wasn't far off."

Jonnie shook her head. "You've got it all wrong, Dan. I wasn't—"

"Don't bother playing this little game any longer, Jonnie. You are, as they say, caught redhanded."

Jonnie's head was pounding and there was a sharp pain behind her eyes. "I could say the same about you, Dan," she replied softly, testing the waters as she invited him to explain the mysterious entries.

All she got in return was a harsh bark of laughter as Dan came toward her, his face darkened. The packages were tossed uncaringly onto the desk, and she watched as the dark coffee spilled over the surface, dripping onto the avocado green carpeting.

"Did you know you've been driving me crazy since you first arrived at Cascades?"

"I'm sorry." Jonnie rose from the chair, backing away from him, the checkbook register forgotten as it fell from her fingers.

The icy mimicry of a smile didn't reach Dan's eyes. "You see, Jonnie," he revealed, his voice a stiletto sheathed in silk. "I was suffering from an attack of guilt. In the beginning, I'd considered using your feelings for me to handle that ridiculous commission. Then you showed up here with that little story that you'd quit. But that was a lie, wasn't it?"

His harsh voice was bitter, and she watched his long fingers thrust through his thick black hair in mute frustration. "I never used to drink much at all. A little beer, a Scotch now and then. But since you walked in the door of my office I've found it a necessary vice. I've drunk enough in the past weeks to drown thoughts of any normal woman. But not you, Jonnie. Not you." He shook his head and his dark-blue eyes pierced her. "Because you're different, aren't you? Very different," he repeated, his voice low and strangely remote.

"Dan, please—"

"Please.... How many times have you asked me that, Jonnie? Please cooperate, Dan. Please trust me,

Dan. Please stay." His mocking tone was spat from twisted lips. "You're just one constant little request line, aren't you, sweetheart?"

Jonnie's control was so brittle, she could feel it threatening to shatter into a million pieces. "Dan, let's talk about this. You wouldn't do anything dishonest. I know you."

"Do you, Jonnie? Which Dan Kincade are you talking about? The hero from your adolescent fantasies? Or the man standing here with you now? The one who breaks your inviolate rules and then lies to you. And we know how you feel about lies, don't we? This is what you wanted, isn't it? You've discovered your damned smoking gun."

As Jonnie watched, his eyes appeared on fire as derision and desire rose to mingle in a heated gleam. "That towel is really quite provocative, sweetheart. What is it about you that I can't help myself from wanting you? Even now."

"It only shows that you're human, with human emotions. I've never expected you to be perfect." Her voice faltered. "Not since I grew up, anyway."

Dan raked his hands through his hair, staring bleakly at the ceiling. Jonnie wanted desperately to bridge the enormous crevasse she felt deepening and widening between them.

"I want you, too, Dan. Doesn't that tell you anything?"

She wanted to tell him of her love. To assure him that whatever he'd done, together they could find a way out of it. Jonnie was trying the words out in her mind when his harsh analysis slashed at her like a knife.

"It only tells me we're two of a kind. I cheat for what I consider a worthwhile purpose, just as you're obviously not above spying for your own easily justifiable ends. And both of us are willing, even, to put those rather shady ideals aside for a few minutes of physical gratification."

Jonnie closed her eyes tightly to the threatening hot tears, refusing to let Dan see her cry. He'd warned her up front that he was incapable of a real relationship. But she hadn't believed it. Behind her closed lids, against a background of swirling black velvet, Jonnie viewed the events of the past ten days. She knew Dan felt something for her. He'd demonstrated it over and over again. How could he not see it himself?

She opened her eyes once again to look at him, faltering slightly as she viewed his hard blue gaze. He was encouraging nothing, she realized. Jonnie took a deep breath, refusing to surrender that easily.

"I don't believe you, Dan. I think you care about me," she argued bravely. "As I care about you."

Love, Jonnie decided at the last moment, was pushing things too far right now. She was trying to draw Dan Kincade closer, not lose him.

"I liked you. And the sex was great. But even if I were willing to consider more, how can you possibly expect anything to come of this when you're doing your damnedest to ruin me? What kind of fool do you think I am?"

He speared her with an angry glare, but Jonnie shook her head firmly, refusing to accept the harsh indictment.

"I'm not trying to ruin you, Dan. It was only an accident. I got your checkbook wet, and was trying to dry it off, and...."

She watched a muscle jump in his cheek, displaying a flash of emotion before his expression turned inscrutable. "What if I were to agree to this relationship, for as long as you wanted, if you were willing to forget you ever saw that check register?"

Jonnie's face paled even whiter at his quietly issued question. "You mean lie? Under oath?"

Dan shrugged. "If necessary, I suppose. You're the one who'd know how much we could get away with, Jonnie."

We, the man had said, putting them in this together. But dear God, she agonized, not this way. She wanted to help him. But this....

"I've sworn to uphold the law, Dan—not break it."

He closed the door on the subject with a weary sigh. "Well, I guess that's that."

His hair was tousled from his long fingers raking through it, and a muscle jerked along his jawline. But it was his eyes—dark and bleak—that captured her attention, holding her to his enigmatic gaze.

"You'd better get dressed, Jonnie. The runway's cleared. We'll be leaving within the hour. That should get you back in time to go shopping for one of those gray serge business suits to wear to my hanging."

Jonnie held out a hand in his direction, not wanting things to end this way.

"Dan, can't we talk about it? Won't you explain?"

He gave a short, harsh sound as he moved to the door. "You're the one with the terrific speech about honor and integrity and rules, counselor. If I recall the conversation correctly, you mentioned something about them being cast in concrete. I admit that I broke your revered regulations. So what the hell do you care why?"

Jonnie moved across the room on unsteady legs. "Dan, please. I'd like to know." Her eyes were misty green pools of need.

"Jonnie, get dressed," Dan almost begged, his voice betraying his unhappiness with the entire situation. "Don't make things worse by asking me to try to explain. It wouldn't do any good."

She gave up, her fingers reaching of their own volition for one last touch of the deep cleft in his chin. "I need to know one thing."

Her voice mustered up a hidden reservoir of strength, and for a brief, fleeting moment Jonnie appeared as the strong, capable woman who first appeared in Dan Kincade's office.

"I'm not promising to tell you anything." His hand was on the doorknob, and Jonnie could tell he wanted nothing more than to escape this room and this conversation. And her.

"If I'd agreed to lie, to hide those checks from the commission...."

"I'd have hated you for turning out to be a fraud," Dan acknowledged in a grave, gritty voice. "Get dressed, Jonnie. I'll meet you down in the lobby."

With that he was gone, leaving her alone in the small hotel room, which at that moment resembled her life. An absolute shambles.

Chapter Twelve

Dan's impassive face could have been carved onto the side of Mount Rushmore for all the expression he revealed on the flight back to Salem. Jonnie's very real fear of flying was replaced by an even greater dread of having lost him. She couldn't think of a single thing to say that would make all this any easier, and even if she could, Dan's attitude certainly didn't invite conversation.

As they entered the terminal, he touched her for the first time, his hands going to her shoulders to push her into a chair. "Wait here while I get your luggage," he instructed, in the tone she'd heard him use to discipline unruly players.

"I can get my own suitcase."

"Don't you dare move from this spot, Ryan, or so help me, I'll throttle you."

Jonnie didn't like the flash of anger in Dan's eyes, but at least it was an improvement over the ice she'd been subjected to during the flight home. Deciding discretion was the better part of valor, she simply nodded her head.

"That's better," he muttered, turning away, his hands thrust into his pockets.

When he returned with her bag, Jonnie walked silently beside him to the parking lot. When she turned toward where she'd left her car, Dan's fingers closed around her elbow.

"You're coming with me."

For a fleeting moment Jonnie wondered if Dan was abducting her in order to keep his secret safe. A moment later, she knew the wild thought was probably born only of her illness. She struggled to maintain an expression of calm, but was too late. From the flare in his blue eyes, she knew Dan had recognized her fear.

"Dammit, I'm not kidnapping you, counselor, so relax. I'm taking you to the emergency room."

"The emergency room? Dan, I don't need to go to the hospital."

"You're sick."

"I've got a winter cold. I get one every year, Dan, it's no big deal."

They'd reached the Blazer, and as he unlocked the passenger door, Dan glared down at her. "Look, lady, I realize you're a hotshot attorney, used to being in charge of everything and everyone. But right now I'm making the decisions, and I say you're going to the emergency room."

He put his hands around her waist, lifting her easily into the front seat. "So why don't you break tradition, Jonnie Ryan, by shutting up and not arguing with me!"

As Dan drove to the hospital, Jonnie tried to make sense of his behavior. The icy silence had settled down about them once again, but she received a small measure of satisfaction from Dan's continuing concern about her health. She had the feeling he was angry because he couldn't dismiss her as easily as he'd like.

Dan continued to display his unwilling concern as he stood silently beside Jonnie, while the clerk filled out a myriad of forms. He remained with her in the sterile confines of the emergency room, only leaving when the doctor finally arrived and ordered him outside.

"I'm going to admit her," the physician told Dan after a lengthy examination.

"I think that's a good idea," Dan agreed. "She's got a lot more than a cold, despite what she keeps insisting."

"Pneumonia, not to mention a severe case of exhaustion," the doctor agreed, nodding his gray head. "She should've seen a doctor days ago."

"She's been busy," Dan muttered, giving Jonnie a glance that would shear the skin off anyone with less internal fortitude. As it was, she was getting sick and tired of the two men talking about her as if she weren't even in the room.

"I don't need to be admitted," she argued, stiffening her back as she sat on the edge of the narrow examining table. "All I need is to go home and get some rest. And eat some chicken soup...with noodles. That always works."

The doctor shook his head, returning his gaze to Dan. "Is the woman always this stubborn? She second-guessed my diagnosis during the entire exam."

"She's usually a lot worse. I don't envy you your job, Doctor." Dan gave Jonnie one long, final look before turning on his heel and going through the double doors.

"Dan, wait!" Jonnie jumped off the table, intent on following him, but she was stopped as the doctor caught her arm, his expression professionally stern.

"You're not going anywhere but to bed, Ms Ryan. And please do us both a favor and sit back down before you fall down. I don't appreciate my patients collapsing on me."

Despite her complaints, Jonnie secretly had to admit that the bed felt marvelous. She was dimly aware of a nurse giving her a shot before she allowed herself to float off to sleep. Her dreams were as they'd been for days, filled with Dan Kincade.

"What in the hell did you think you were doing?" Dan's palms were pressed against the oak surface of the desk as he leaned toward the older man. Every taut line in his body demonstrated that he was only maintaining control through rigid self-discpline.

"We've worked together for a long time, E.G.," he continued. "You were assistant coach under Tom Ryan when I played here. How in the hell could you throw me to the wolves this way?"

The older man shook his head, obviously not anymore pleased with the situation than Dan Kincade. "I told you, Dan, when this thing first started that it was a matter of priorities—the greater good for the greater number. I had to consider your actions against what would happen to Cascade's reputation."

"So I was suddenly expendable. You can always get another basketball coach, but cushy administrative jobs are harder to come by, aren't they?"

The man flinched at Dan's accusation and waved his hand in the direction of a chair. "Sit down son, and let's talk this out."

"I'm not your son. And there's nothing to talk out!" It was a roar that could very well have come from a wounded lion. Dan relented after his outburst, sinking down into the offered chair.

"It's not just me, E.G. Did you think about the repercussions for Bishop and Anne? Did you think what this could do to her?"

"You should have thought of them in the beginning, Dan."

Dan pounded one strong fist into his palm, looking ready to explode. "I did think of them, dammit. That's what all this was about."

"It was a personal decision you made, Dan. I told you it was going to have to be that way if it came out."

"It didn't come out, E.G. You volunteered it to that snake Morrison sent down to talk to you, while he had Jonnie Ryan keeping me busy."

"If he was fishing Dan, he sure acted like he knew exactly where the granddaddy trout was hiding out. Do you believe that?"

The question startled Dan out of his smoldering anger for a moment. "Do I believe what?"

"That the Ryan girl was using her relationship with you. As I recall you're the one who stood in this very office denying that claim when I suggested its possibility."

Dan rose, confusion written on his face. "I don't know what I believe about anything anymore."

His eyes roamed the ceiling, as if hoping to find answers emblazoned on the white plaster. When none were forthcoming, he returned his gaze to the quietly watching man.

"I do know I feel a helluva lot like the guy on 'Mission Impossible' who's just realized the agency really *will* disavow any knowledge of his existence."

With that he turned and walked down the hall to his own office, where he began emptying his desk.

"It's about time you woke up."

Jonnie offered a pleased, wobbly smile at the tall, silver-haired man standing at the foot of her bed.

"Dad, what are you doing here?"

"Dan called me and told me what fool stunts you were up to these days. You scared us all to death, young lady—although you do look a lot better than when I arrived last night."

She leaned up on her elbows, gazing slowly around the room.

"That's good to hear. I was afraid I might've died. I see you've already sent out the invitations to the wake." She grinned at the five men whose large bodies were contorted into the small, hard vinyl chairs— five men who all resembled one another in varying degrees, as they resembled her.

"Helluva place to hold a family reunion, sprout."

Jason Ryan leaned over the bed, gathering his sister into his arms for a brief hug. He was followed in order by Greg, Tyler, Patrick and finally Tom Ryan.

This was what Jonnie had always loved about being a part of a large family. If one was in trouble, the others rallied around immediately and closed ranks. They protected their own, the Ryan clad did. She wondered who was protecting Dan right now.

"Dan called you?"

"He did. He's really concerned, honey. He made me promise to keep him advised on your condition. In fact, he was pacing these hallways like a caged wolf until it got too bad with the press and all." The brown eyes, dark under the slash of silver brows, narrowed in recollection. "At the time, it was difficult to tell which of you was worse off. He looks terrible."

A lone wolf, she considered sadly, that's what the stubborn man insisted on being. Jonnie expelled a short, shallow breath, surprised as it caused a slight stab of pain.

Her father didn't miss her slight grimace. "Running around in all that bad weather, topped off by spending thirty hours in an airport and all that stress wasn't exactly what the doctor ordered, kiddo. You're just fortunate Dan was around to take care of you."

"He did take care of me," she acknowledged. "But that was before he believed I was going to destroy him."

There was a murmur of male voices, and Tom Ryan acted as spokesman, correcting her softly, but insistently. "No, it was after he realized that. Dan's no dummy, Jonnie. I suspect he knew his goose was cooked the moment you walked into his office."

"Then why—" The conversation was deftly halted by the appearance of the nurse, arriving with a hypodermic needle on her tray.

"I feel like a pincushion," Jonnie complained, rubbing her sore bottom as the nurse left them alone with stern instructions for Jonnie to rest and not attempt to rush her recovery.

"That's an improvement. I spent last night watching them shoot penicillin into you without hearing one single word of complaint. Knowing what a big baby you are about needles, that worried me more than anything else. Never knew you not to be a fighter, honey."

"I don't know," Greg Ryan drawled, grinning down at her with all the teasing of a brother who was a mere fifteen months older. "I thought it was kind of nice for a change. I used to get damned embarrassed when we'd all go in for our booster shots, and Jonnie would start screaming bloody murder."

She waved her fist threateningly. "You just wait until I get out of this bed, Gregory James Ryan. I'll bloody murder you."

The burst of temper made everyone laugh, including Jonnie. Because she was the closest in age to Greg, their entire relationship had been one of friendly competition. She loved him, though, and wouldn't have it any other way.

And it was the truth; Jonnie did hate needles. She could still recall the frustration of being in first grade and told by the school nurse as they all lined up for those shots that she was too big a girl to cry. All the other little girls had been allowed to bawl their heads off. But, of course, they'd been blond and petite.

Only Jason had come over to her on the playground, giving her his best aggie shooter and telling her to ignore the dummies and cry if she wanted. Even at six, Jonnie had realized that whatever she did in life, Jason would always be there to smooth out the edges. She only wished life could be solved with the gift of a favorite marble these days.

"All right, you guys," her father's gruff voice interrupted the sibling teasing as he noted the sadness on Jonnie's pale face. "It's time to let your sister get some rest. Why don't you all get out of here and get something to eat. Something that doesn't taste like that plastic we've been eating downstairs in the hospital cafeteria."

The initial complaints about leaving her soon developed into a heated discussion over what to eat. As they left the room, still arguing, pizza seemed to be running neck and neck with steak.

It was odd how quiet things were suddenly. Jonnie had forgotten how when the family was together the energy level in a room seemed to increase dramatically. She loved her brothers dearly, but it was nice to be alone with her father.

"Oh, dad. I've made such a mess of things."

Her father was instantly by her side, taking her hand in his own larger one, dark brown eyes filled with paternal love.

"No, honey," he argued. "I think you both have. But it isn't too late to fix things."

Jonnie turned her head away from his warm, sympathetic gaze and buried her face into her pillow, tears dampening the starched material of the cover.

"You don't know," she mumbled.

"About the illegal payments?"

She turned her head back toward him, the swift movement causing her pain. "How did you find out about them? They were made from his personal checkbook. It was only an accident that I discovered them in the first place."

Jonnie watched Tom Ryan nod, as if something had just clicked into place. "That explains it," he murmured, almost to himself, as his eyes left hers to gaze out the window. He appeared intent on the silvery drizzle typical of the long Oregon winter.

"Did Dan tell you everything?"

"Didn't tell me a thing." Tom Ryan pulled a chair up to her bed and sat down. He held out a glass of water and Jonnie drank long and thirstily from the bent straw.

"Thanks, dad."

She leaned her head back onto the pillow, deciding the nurse had been right about not rushing things. Just that little exercise with the glass seemed to leave her feeling as weak as a kitten.

"If he didn't tell you anything, how do you know he's in trouble?"

Her father's dark eyes surveyed her with the gravity of a parent attempting to do the best thing for his child. Jonnie appreciated his efforts, but there was someone else involved in all this. Someone she loved and was not about to desert. Even if the man was too damn stubborn to admit that not even he could get through life entirely alone.

"Dad, please. I'll just worry if you don't come clean. And that can't be good for me," she coaxed.

The long hand covered hers on the sheet, his fingers entwining with hers. "It seems that while you were with Dan in Denver, William Murdock sent down another investigator, Jeff Scott."

Jonnie nodded. She'd worked with Jeff before. He was good at his job. Like a shark seeking out blood in the water, Jeff Scott was unceasingly vigilant and brutally vicious. She'd seen him throw out two or three feelers—guesses, nothing more—and have a witness rattling off facts and figures like a high-speed computer. She knew he couldn't have pulled that successfully with Dan Kincaid. It must have been Brian Bishop who'd tipped him off.

"He seems to have managed to uncover the existence of some illegal funds."

"What has Dan said?"

"Nothing."

The answer brought her eyes wide open with a jolt. "What do you mean, nothing?"

Tom Ryan shrugged. "Exactly that. Oh, he's admitted that he may have been unwise extending loans to certain players, but he won't name names. And he refuses to explain why he did it."

Jonnie shook her head, wondering if it was her illness that was making all this so difficult to comprehend.

"Dad, the name was written in the register. I don't understand."

"You said you found the entries in his personal checkbook?" Her father's deep voice held a question.

"That's right. He'd left it on the desk in the room and I...."

Jonnie's voice drifted off, and she blushed slightly at the thought of her father knowing she'd been in a hotel room with Dan. They both knew she was an adult, for heaven's sake, but there were still a few things Jonnie realized she was uncomfortable discussing with her father.

But Tom Ryan paid no attention to the intimation of her relationship with Dan. His mind was on something else.

"I thought that might be the explanation. Scott got a search-and-seizure order and went through every file in Dan's office with a fine-tooth comb. They haven't been able to come up with a single conclusive piece of evidence against him."

Jonnie felt a deep pain of regret that Dan was having to go through all this. Why hadn't he told her? He'd been concealing his actions since the beginning. How long could their relationship have continued that way, based on a tissue of lies?

"How are they managing to accuse him without any evidence?"

"Harrison." Her father's retort accompanied a snort of irritation. "I always thought that guy was too cautious, even as a coach. He apparently got rattled by the investigation and mentioned something to Scott about whatever funds Dan may have given players being a personal decision. He disavowed any knowledge of which players, or why, but the statement was enough to pique Scott's interest.

"Remember, the commission isn't subject to the strict guidelines of a court appearance," her father pointed out. "They got Dan in the hearing room this morning and tossed out the question, obviously hoping they could uncover some physical evidence of misconduct in the meantime. Everyone seemed stunned when Dan readily admitted making the payments."

"Under oath," Jonnie breathed softly.

She remembered what he'd said about hating her if she'd been willing to lie for him, to cover up. Whatever he'd done, Dan Kincade was honest. She knew it. There had to be a reason that wouldn't fit into the black-and-white regulations. Her previously sacrosanct rules, Jonnie derided herself silently.

That's what Dan had been attempting to tell her that first night at dinner—that they were all answerable to a higher authority than her commission. He'd been willing to follow his conscience on this matter, even when it put his reputation in jeopardy. And now she was not at all surprised to learn he was stonewalling in order to protect someone he considered an innocent victim.

"Dad, I've got to get to the hearing," Jonnie suddenly announced, struggling to push the sheets away.

"No way, kiddo. You're staying right there in that bed until the doctor releases you."

Jonnie observed her father's drawn face and realized she'd caused him a great deal of worry. But this was so very important.

"Then will you at least promise me you'll keep track of what's happening to Dan?"

Her father shook his head. "That won't be hard. The poor guy keeps calling every few hours. He's really been out of his mind over you."

At one time, Jonnie could only have viewed Dan's concern as worry about his own situation, wondering whether she would give the commission evidence they were seeking. A Jonnie Ryan who was only capable of seeing life with simplistic clarity could have ascribed those motives to his behavior.

But now she knew Dan Kincade—and herself—
better. She realized without a single, lingering doubt
that his worrying about her, in the midst of all his
problems, was proof of his love.

She really was feeling better, Jonnie considered,
eyeing her father asleep in the chair a few minutes
later. He was dead to the world. Knowing her father,
she'd bet anything he'd been hovering over her since
his arrival hours ago.

It was time for the news, and Jonnie pointed the remote control toward the darkened television screen,
putting in her earphone so as not to disturb her father. The local broadcast's lead story was, quite naturally, the Murdock Commission. She listened with
increasing dread to the report and viewed the chalk
sketches rendered by the artist covering the hearings.
Even with the exaggerated details by the courtroom
artist, Dan looked terrible.

His emergence from the courthouse only served to
reinforce the drawings. His cheekbones were unusu-
ally prominent, his eyes sunken hollows, dark shadows like angry bruises highly visible on her color
screen. His gruff "no comment" as he made his way
through the throng of reporters only contributed to his
image of a man who was neck deep in hot water and
in danger of going under at any moment.

Jonnie slid a cautious glance over to her father, then
carefully pulled back the covers. She found her
clothes, and although they were wrinkled from having been slept in on the plane, they'd have to do. She
dressed in the bathroom, taking time to write her fa-

ther a short explanatory note. Then she left the room, moved stealthily past the nurses' station and dashed out the hospital doors.

Fortunately there was a cab parked outside, and she climbed into the back seat, giving the driver her destination. Her car, she realized, must still be parked in the airport long-term lot. Jonnie hated to imagine what it would cost to recover it after all this time, especially since she had an unwelcome premonition that she'd be unemployed tomorrow morning.

"This is quite unusual, you realize, Ms Ryan."

Judge Warner invited Jonnie into his home, directing her toward a chair in his book-filled study. "Is there a particular reason why you couldn't submit your request through more normal channels?"

Jonnie noted belatedly that the man's dinner jacket and black bow tie were far too formal attire for a man to wear while relaxing on a quiet evening at home. She'd been too nervous when the cab had driven up to fully grasp the significance of the crush of cars parked on both sides of the street outside this roomy Edwardian home, but awareness now dawned. She'd crashed a party, obviously, something she'd never think of doing under normal conditions. But at this point, she was far beyond worrying about bending a few social rules.

Jonnie had already left the hospital without authorization, and if Judge Warner would just agree, she had every intention of shattering several tenets far more serious than those of polite etiquette.

"I realize that, Your Honor," she answered with a soft, coaxing smile. "But I've been ill and unable to get to my office. The Murdock Commission needs the records I can provide. And by tomorrow I can't guarantee Mr. Kincade will still have them available."

That was an out and out lie. Jonnie knew Dan would never destroy the checkbook register. But she needed to play her only ace. She knew it wouldn't take William Murdock or Jeff Scott long to realize they were looking in the wrong place. She had to get to that checkbook before they did.

"All right," he agreed. "I'm all in favor of integrity in our collegiate sports, having played a little college football myself in the old days."

He smiled with amusement, and as he moved to his desk Jonnie noted that for a man well into his sixties he was still in very good physical form. While she doubted that football was his game any longer, he obviously exercised regularly. She smiled inwardly, remembering Dan's comment about everyone in Eugene jogging.

It was true. Oregonians all seemed to consider inactivity a cardinal sin. The outdoor life and sports predominated from the urban atmosphere of Portland, which lay in the shadow of Mt. Hood's ski resorts, to the small communities on the southern border, remote pockets of the Cascade Mountain range, meccas for hunting and fishing.

Jonnie worked to control the elation she was feeling as she watched the judge begin filling out her search warrant. Signing it with a bold, dark scrawl, he handed it to her.

"Here you go, young lady, signed, sealed and delivered. I don't mind working at home, but see you don't make a habit of bursting in on my anniversary parties."

"Anniversary?"

He nodded a leonine head. "Forty-five years—to the same woman." His tone held both pride and incredulity, and Jonnie leaned forward to give him a quick, highly unprofessional peck on his weathered cheek.

"That's wonderful. And to pay you back for this, Judge Warner, make a note in your appointment book. You're invited to my forty-fifth anniversary party."

"Are you married, Ms Ryan?" he inquired as she headed toward the door.

Jonnie looked back over her shoulder, giving the judge an absolutely dazzling smile. "Not yet, Your Honor. But keep your pen handy. I'm going to be needing a marriage license any day."

Then she surprised them both with a huge wink, which was totally at odds with the sophisticated young woman she appeared to be.

Jonnie had kept the cab waiting, and as she slid into the back seat she gave the driver another address. Then she lifted the precious white paper to her lips for a brief, happy kiss.

"Lady, you gotta be kidding. That's sixty miles away."

"Sixty-two," she answered calmly. "But who's counting?"

"I am. That's a helluva long cab ride."

"Tell me, Mr.—" she leaned forward to read the name on the license "—Madison, do you get many fares on a night like this?"

"Are you kidding? Anyone with the sense God gave to a duck is inside on a night like tonight. This rain'd choke a mallard."

He'd turned around in the front seat, eyeing her carefully. The expression on his red, beefy face indicated to Jonnie that he suspected she might be an escaped inmate from the state mental hospital on the other side of Salem.

"Then you should be delighted about a two-way trip to Eugene. One hundred and twenty-four miles, Mr. Madison, all which will be tallied on that cute little meter."

Jonnie sat back, folded her arms and smiled serenely as she waited for him to restart the engine.

"Are you expecting any trouble?" The huskier of the two deputies Jonnie had brought with her to help serve the paper on Dan dropped his hand instinctively to the service revolver he wore low on his hip.

"Good Lord, no! So please don't worry about using that." She cast a weak, wary glance at the seemingly enormous handgun. "We'll be in and out before that coffee I dragged you away from back at the station can get cold."

Dan opened his door, his eyes widening with surprise as he saw Jonnie standing on his front porch. For a long, silent moment he studied her, his blue eyes uncensored and loving as he drank in her pallid features, as if searching for a hint to her health. Then his startled gaze moved to the two uniformed men behind her, and a jet-black brow arched before lowering to join the other in a harsh, angry line.

"Miss Ryan," he said formally. "I suppose you're inviting yourself in."

Jonnie had been making her own study of the chiseled features of his face, noting the lines that had not been there days before. His mouth was pulled in a tight hard line, and his eyes had turned to blue ice. One eye, she noted, was swollen, and the skin around it a mottled purple, almost as if he'd been hit. His scathing tone jerked her mind away from her appraisal, back to the matter at hand.

"I am, Dan," she said softly, wishing fervently that she could blink twice and make her accomplices disappear to allow a private moment with him. There was so much to say, so much to explain. But it would have to wait.

"Tom and his four musketeers will be relieved to know you've recovered enough to go back to work protecting innocent citizens of Oregon from corruption," he stated on a flat, accusing note.

"Dad called you?"

"Several times. Jason even drove down here looking for his runaway sister. You just missed him." Dan's tone was dry, his eyes crystal blue glass. "They had the strange idea you'd show up here because you cared."

Jonnie watched helplessly as he raked his long fingers through his soft black curls. "To tell you the truth," he admitted, "so did I. It just goes to show how dumb a guy can be when he makes the mistake of falling in love with a reformer, doesn't it?"

He'd said it! Jonnie's heart seemed to take flight at his seemingly unconscious revelation. Her soaring senses returned to earth with a jolt, however, as she remembered the circumstances of her visit. As if on cue, one of the deputies behind her nervously cleared his throat, awaiting instructions.

Jonnie held out the paper, her hands betraying her as they trembled slightly. "I've brought—"

"I know," Dan cut in. "You're here for the checkbook."

Jonnie could only nod, hating the look she saw mirrored in eyes which had once regarded her with such tenderness.

"It's in the top drawer of the desk in the bedroom." Dan stepped aside to allow the uninvited trio to enter. I think I'll stay here. I'm sure you can remember the way, counselor."

His cold tone slashed at her like winter sleet. It was all Jonnie could do to keep from flinging her arms around that strong neck and crying out how much she loved him, assuring him that she'd never, ever hurt him.

Instead she simply nodded, keeping her eyes to the floor as she led the men to the room, where she located the damning piece of evidence precisely where Dan had told her she'd find it.

She had intended to leave immediately upon retrieving the checkbook, but one look at Dan's haggard face had her altering her plan. She had so little time. But she couldn't leave like this.

She thanked the two deputies as they prepared to return to the station in their patrol car, asking them to tell the driver of the cab she'd be just a few more minutes. Then she turned back to Dan. He hadn't said a word, but something flickered in his eyes, momentarily, that she couldn't recognize.

"You came down here in a cab? All the way from Salem?"

Jonnie nodded. "My car was at the airport. I didn't want to take the time to pick it up."

"A real eager beaver, aren't you? It's really something to see you in action, Jonnie. You were quite impressive, the way you had those two goons just waiting for instructions. Would they have handcuffed me and thrown me into the back of that squad car if you'd given the word, too?" His eyes narrowed dangerously. "How much power have you managed to grasp hold of in your short political life?"

Jonnie tempered the flare of anger, knowing that she had no energy to lose on useless emotions. She had too much work yet to do tonight to blow it on an argument based on Dan's misconceptions of the situation. Instead, she met his derisive gaze steadily.

"Do you have any steak in the house?"

A jet brow arched inquisitively. "Feel the need for a little raw meat, counselor? I'd think you could wait until you throw me to the lions tomorrow for that."

She bit her bottom lip to stop the retort that was aching to spring forth. Damn him anyway. He sure wasn't making it easy. Dan was damn lucky she understood he was striking out from pain, not hatred, or she'd show him a thing or two.

"I was thinking more in terms of that eye. Whatever did you do to it?"

"I walked into a door."

Dan flinched visibly as Jonnie reached up to trace her fingers around the swelling flesh. "It looks horrible and it's getting worse. You need to put something on it—if not steak, at least some ice."

She walked in the direction of the kitchen, but Dan grasped her hand, turning her back toward him.

"Don't do that," he ordered.

She gazed down pointedly to where his long fingers encircled her wrist. "You're going to leave a bruise, Dan."

"Then leave," he suggested, his tone uneven and desperately harsh. "Don't put any ice on my eye. Don't worry about it. And don't pretend you care when you don't. You've done enough, Jonnie. Let it go.... Leave me alone. Get back to your career, your commission and your goddamn rules of honor."

He flung her hand down, turning away from her. Jonnie hated to see the slump of those wide shoulders, and the downcast tilt of his head, but she knew there was nothing she could do about it now. She didn't have time to explain to Dan about her plan. And she knew he couldn't trust her enough to simply tell her the truth and let her take matters from there.

"I'll see you tomorrow," she said softly, turning away from the silent, brooding man.

"I've not a single doubt about it, Jonnie. I sure hope it's worth it to you."

Her cheeks flared an unnatural pink in her ashen pallor, but Dan missed it. "Oh, it is," Jonnie assured him as she opened the front door, knowing they were talking about two entirely different things.

Daniel Kincade was the most frustratingly closed man she'd ever met. Beginning tomorrow she was going to start changing that, if it took the next fifty years.

Jonnie made a dash through the torrential rain, returning to the now-familiar back seat of the cab, and gave the driver one more address. *The key,* Jonnie considered, leaning her head back against the vinyl seat.

Chapter Thirteen

Certainly not for the first time in her life, Jonnie was glad to be a member of a large family as she watched her father and brothers digging through their billfolds and pockets to come up with the cab fare. It had been an expensive night, thus far, and the real work was just beginning.

"I don't know whether to kiss you or kill you," Tom Ryan said as they sat around her kitchen table. "You've been driving us all crazy. Jason even drove down to Eugene to see if you'd shown up at Dan's."

"I know, he told me. You're right, by the way, dad. Dan looks horrible. And his eye, you should see what he did to himself...."

The silence suddenly became a living thing, swirling about them. Jonnie's eyes moved from her father around the circle of faces to her eldest brother, whose hands were hidden under the table top.

"Jason, you wouldn't have...." Jonnie's eyes widened, and she shook her head, disbelieving herself capable of such a thought. But as he reddened uncomfortably, the dark flush rising from his collar over his face, her suspicions were increased. She reached out and tugged at his arms.

"You didn't!" She ran her fingers over the bruised knuckles of his left hand, and her eyes flew to his chagrined face. "Jason Ryan, you really did hit Dan, didn't you?"

A grunt was the only answer she received, and Jonnie wondered why she was suddenly finding the entire scenario so silly. She laughed, the release expelling a lot of suppressed tension.

"You're the one Jason should've hit," Greg broke in with a wicked grin. "Why don't you let me do it, Dad? Jonnie always has needed to be turned over someone's knee."

"You just try it, Greg Ryan, and I'll make mincemeat of that pretty face you're always gazing at in the mirror."

Greg was the best-looking of the Ryan men and more than a little vain. Jonnie knew her jibe had struck home when he glared at her with brotherly disdain.

"I agree with Greg."

Jonnie's head spun toward the two quietest of her brothers, Patrick and Tyler, who'd spoken in unison. While the twins never had been her defenders, like Jason, they'd never tormented her like Greg. They usually smiled at anything she ever did or said, appearing to approve wholehertetedly of whatever outrageous behavior Jonnie had chosen to exhibit. She couldn't believe they would side against her.

"Well, dammit, Jonnie, you had us all worried sick," Patrick complained.

"It's not always easy, being your cheering section, but this latest trick was too much." Tyler added his two cents to the conversation.

She could only look at the stern expressions on the five male faces and agree. If she had been in their place, she'd have been going crazy. But the ends justify the means, she reminded herself quietly.

"I apologize to one and all," she said, with unaccustomed humility. "My only excuse was I was trying to help someone we all love." Her eyes moved around the silent circle, asking contrition as well as understanding. "We do all love Dan, don't we?"

Jason rubbed his hand ruefully, but the murmured chorus was unanimous in its agreement.

"Good." Before their eyes, she became the brisk, competent attorney, pulling out the ledgers she'd acquired at her last stop in Eugene. "I've got some figures for each of you to go over. I want to match up all these receipts with Dan's checkbook register."

"This'll take all night," Greg moaned.

"That's right," she answered. "I'll put on the coffee, and we'll all get started." She thought for a moment. "Dad, why don't you go on to bed? We can handle everything."

"The hell I will, Jonnie Ryan. You're not the only one who cares about that hardheaded man."

"This is ridiculous. You've got your fever back from all that running around in the rain yesterday. And then staying up all those hours last night.... What do I have to do—tie you down?"

Tom Ryan shook down the mercury in the thermometer, eyeing Jonnie with fatherly concern. He looked every bit like a man about to lay down the law—if he could only figure out how to make it stick.

"Sorry, dad. But I'll have loads of time to recuperate. I'm young and strong. A little cold certainly won't kill me."

"Pneumonia," he reminded her grimly. "And that well could, young lady."

"Pooh, only old people die of pneumonia, and I'm not old."

"You sure couldn't tell that from the looks of you," Greg countered, entering the room and finding his way to the coffeepot. His brown gaze moved over her tall, too-thin frame. "You look like walking death."

"She does not," Patrick responded, with that automatic approval he'd always held for his sister. Well, almost always, Jonnie allowed, remembering his uncharacteristic show of resistance last night. "She looks fine, doesn't she, Jason?"

"Somewhere in between," her eldest brother answered soberly, his eyes warming her as they followed the same path Patrick's had taken, with more honesty. "You don't look like you died last week, but you're not exactly at your best, honey."

She smiled her thanks. She could always count on Jason to be honest and straight shooting with her.

Next to Dan, she probably loved Jason Ryan the best of any individual in the entire world.

"A little blusher will work wonders. Don't worry." Jonnie choked on her coffee, finding it too hot in her rush to get ready for the hearing.

"Pneumonia," her father muttered, shaking his head.

"Burned tongue," she countered, kissing him on the top of his head as she rose from the table. "Have some faith in your daughter, pop."

Tom Ryan realized why he'd begun getting these silver hairs as Jonnie entered her teens. There was probably one on his head for every argument she'd ever given him. He smiled to himself in spite of his worry, thinking that Dan Kincade didn't stand a chance.

Although she'd never admit it to her father, or her brothers, Jonnie felt far shakier than she had yesterday, as if she'd borrowed too deeply from her store of energy.

"Just a few short hours," she told herself, trying out some rose tint brushed high on her cheekbones. "Then you can go back to bed, pull the covers over your head and sleep this stupid old thing right out of your body."

Pep talk over, she glued a reassuring smile on her face and returned to take her father's arm as they left for the courthouse.

Not long after they arrived, she heard a familiar voice exclaim, "Jonnie Ryan, aren't you a sight for sore eyes!"

Jonnie had been standing in the corridor, waiting for Jason as he parked the car. Her position on the commission had gotten Tom and her brothers admitted to a special hearing room with a closed-circuit camera so they could view the proceedings. The one thing she'd never counted on was seeing Michael Cunningham again—and certainly not today.

"You're looking well, Michael," she stated quietly, coolly appraising the tall, handsome man. His blond hair was thick and combed in a style that complemented his boyishly handsome face. His Arizona tan was a glorious bronze foil for his golden hair, and his blue eyes were guileless as they met her sea-green gaze.

"You're looking better than well, Jonnie, honey. You look absolutely gorgeous. Never better."

"What are you doing here?"

"Looking for the most gorgeous woman in Oregon."

"Knock it off, Michael. Why are you really here?" Jonnie had neither the energy nor the inclination for flirting with this irresponsible man.

"I'm back on investigative reporting for News-View Magazine. This story has been getting a lot of national press, and since I covered a few juicy athletic scandals in Arizona, I thought I'd see what I could do with this one."

Jonnie considered slapping his handsome face as he grinned. "There's nothing the folks like better than to watch a saint fall off his pedestal, Jonnie." He winked with wicked insinuation. "But you should know all about that, since you're the one doing the pushing."

"You need to review your facts, Michael. You've got this story dead wrong."

"Maybe you can clear up a few things for me, then," he said smoothly, reminding Jonnie once again that no matter how she felt about Michael Cunningham personally, he was still the press and she should watch her step.

She headed toward the door to the hearing room, deciding Jason could simply ask a guard here to find the rest of the family. How difficult would it be to locate four men all over six foot five?

"I've missed you, Jonnie." She was stopped by a hand on her arm.

"Perhaps if you spent more time with your wife, you'd have less time to think about me," she responded briskly.

"Danielle isn't my wife any longer."

Jonnie wasn't surprised. If Michael acted like this every time he left town, a woman would have two choices. Tie him down or divorce him.

"Really?" she asked with disinterest, looking past his shoulder as she finally spotted Jason heading their way.

"Well, almost not," he admitted with a sheepish grin that at one time Jonnie had found irresistible. "We're going to get a divorce as soon as we find the time to hash out the settlement."

Sure, Jonnie thought. He'd never change. And what was more, she didn't care one way or another.

"Well, it was nice talking with you, Michael, but I have to get inside."

The tanned fingers tightened on her wrist. "Look Jonnie, don't act like this. I told you the truth this time, didn't I? I haven't forgotten how that was such a big deal with you.

"So I'm married. We're both adults. We can still get together and talk about old times, can't we? Rekindle a few sparks with an old flame?"

"And see what scoop you might be able to get on the story? Honestly, Michael, you're too much. I never told you anything last time, and I'll be damned if I discuss a terrific man like Dan Kincade with the likes of you."

Her eyes hardened to jade agates as she stared pointedly at his fingers, still on her sleeve. "Now, if you'll let go of me, I do have to get to work."

"This guy bothering you, Jonnie?"

Jonnie could've bust into laughter at the sheer fright that etched its way onto Michael's face as he spun around to look a long, long way up into Jason Ryan's glowering countenance. Dan had been right. Jason was an intimidating presence.

"I was just explaining to this gentlemen that I had to get to work," she explained. "Everything's fine, Jason."

"You sure?"

Jonnie allowed a longer than necessary pause as she studied Michael slowly, delighting in his discomfort.

"I'm sure," she decided. She nodded at Michael. "Goodbye, Michael. It's been—uh—interesting."

"Who was that?" Jason asked as they watched Michael retreat, reminding Jonnie somewhat of a crab scuttling away in the sand.

"A ghost of foolishness past," she murmured, wondering what had ever made her think she cared one iota for the man.

"He hurt you." It wasn't a question, and Jonnie knew better than to lie to her brother.

"He did. But it was a long time ago."

"I should've belted him."

Jonnie laughed heartily as she went up on her toes to kiss away her brother's scowl.

"You keep defending me like this, brother dear, and you'll punch yourself right out of the NBA. You old guys can only take so much abuse, you know. Save the fighting for under the basket."

"I was told you'd be unavailable for another week, at least." William Murdock greeted Jonnie's arrival at his table without a great deal of warmth. "I suspected you were covering up for Kincade." His dark eyes made a detailed study of her. "But you look like hell. So I guess you really were sick, huh?"

"I was," Jonnie agreed dryly. "And thanks for the uplifting words. It's always nice for a woman to know she looks her best."

"You left us up the proverbial creek, Jonnie. We started this entire questioning without knowing where the hell the man was hiding those funds."

"You're the one who dropped the paddle, William, when you decided Scott's methods were more effective than mine. All he managed to do was wring some innuendos from a man who never has been known to possess an iron spine. What kind of evidence is that?''

"Not good," he acknowledged. "But the press was on our backs, not to mention the governor, and I had to come up with something. So I decided to get Kincade on the stand and let him lie. That way once we found the funds, we could prove he was a liar as well as a corrupt coach.''

"But he isn't a liar, is he?" Jonnie turned her head to observe Dan as he entered the room.

"He may not be," William Murdock muttered under his breath, following her gaze to the steely blue eyes that were regarding them both as if they were a matched pair of rattlesnakes. "But he sure as hell is a crook, Ryan. I know it. All I have to do is give Scott more time to sniff out the proof."

Jonnie leaned back in her chair, lacing her fingers together as she linked them behind her neck. She rotated her head in lazy circles, attempting to banish the headache that had been growing with throbbing intensity since late last night.

It had taken her family hours to match up all the receipts the bishops had given her with the amounts deducted in Dan's checkbook register. But finally, before dawn had broken, every last cent had been accounted for.

"I can go Jeff Scott one better," she offered, turning a bland gaze toward her boss and political mentor, her pulse jumping rapidly as she made her move. "I'll present the evidence to the jury this morning for you."

It was not often Jonnie Ryan had seen William lose control of the suave urbanity he wore like a second skin. His dark eyes widened, his mouth dropped open, and for a fleeting moment the consummate politician had all the charisma of a grounded trout.

"You'd better not be kidding about this, Ryan," he warned.

"I'm not."

He held out a perfectly manicured hand. "Then let me see it."

Jonnie held her ground and shook her tawny head. "Uh-uh. This one is mine."

His gaze narrowed suspiciously, and Jonnie hoped he couldn't tell she was holding her breath. "What in hell do you mean by that? Do I need to remind you that you work for me?"

"I thought I was forced to take a leave of absence," she reminded him.

"For your health," he reminded her, lying through his teeth. *But he does it so well,* she marveled, almost admiring the ability. "I was afraid if you kept driving yourself, Jonnie, you'd end up in the hospital, as you did. I was only worried about you."

"I thought that was all it was," she murmured, keeping her eyes lowered so he couldn't view her excitement as she worked to draw him further into the trap he'd helped set for himself. "But I want to be the one to have Daniel Kincade on the stand when I reveal where the money went." She purposely misled him, crossing her fingers behind her neck. "I've earned it, William. Believe me."

A sly smile crossed his handsome features. "So it's true what they say about a woman scorned." Jonnie watched with well-concealed tenseness as his smooth brow furrowed. "But it's my commission, Ryan, and my upcoming campaign. All evidence belongs to me."

She'd been prepared for this objection. "Of course that's true. But we've already read far too many allegations that you only appointed me to this commission because of our supposed personal relationship." Jonnie smiled, encouraging cooperation. "Just think how your opponents would be forced to drop that tactic if I were to prove myself a competent, intelligent investigator."

Jonnie watched the wheels turning as William tested out different scenarios, including the one she'd just handed him. It had to be her, she breathed a silent prayer. Because she knew he'd never call Ann Bishop up there once he knew the facts.

"All right," he decided finally.

Jonnie smiled her thanks, motioning toward the deputy who'd been waiting by the closed door. The uniformed officer came forward, handing her the file.

"Remind me never to get tangled up with you personally, Ryan," William said to her in a low voice as she called Dan Kincade to the witness stand. "You're about as treacherous as a black widow spider."

"You've taught me well, William," she answered smoothly, her expression becoming more serious as Dan was reminded by the clerk that he was still under oath.

"Mr. Kincade," Jonnie began the encounter briskly, her voice cool and professional, "you've told this commission that you knowingly extended unauthorized funds to certain student athletes. Is that information true?"

There was a hint of a mocking smile at the corner of Dan's full mouth. "If I were going to lie, Miss Ryan, surely I'd be more likely to assert that I hadn't loaned those funds. It wouldn't do me a lot of good to say I had—if I hadn't."

There was a tittering from the supposedly impartial jury, and Jonnie was pleased to see that at least they were starting out on their side—Dan's and hers. This was without a doubt the strangest situation she'd ever found herself in. It was as if she had, during her years as deputy prosecutor, suddenly switched sides and started arguing for the defense.

Jonnie knew that when all was said and done, her political career would probably be over. The party was not wild about turncoats, especially those who'd pull a stunt like this. But Dan had been right from the beginning. This had been organized by a handful of self-serving individuals as nothing but a political lynching party. And unusual circumstances called for unusual measures.

"Coach Kincade," she continued, "could you please give us the name or names of any players who received money from you?"

"No." Dan's jaw was firm, his eyes steady as they willingly met her gaze. "I couldn't."

"I see. You realize you could be held in contempt of this commission?"

Dan's eyes relayed the fact that he already held a vast amount of contempt for Jonnie Ryan's treasured commission.

"I do."

Jonnie lowered her head for a moment, ruffling through some papers in the manila folder. She knew exactly what the file held. And she knew that Dan also knew. But theatrics were often as much a part of the legal system as jurisprudence, and she was playing them for all they were worth.

"Would you recall the name if you heard it?" she asked patiently, her gaze as smooth as spun silk.

"I might."

"What would you say, Coach Kincade, if I suggested that you'd extended those loans to a certain graduating guard on the team? Brian Bishop, I believe?"

Dan abruptly dropped the pretense of cool aloofness. "I'd say you should all be ashamed of yourselves. You're dragging a lot of personal grief through this closed room, leaking whatever you might find politically beneficial to that mob of leeches out there."

Jonnie wondered idly how Michael would like being referred to as a leech. She had to fight the smile from breaking loose on her lips.

Dan's hands curled into fists, and his furious steel-blue gaze moved around the room, taking in what he obviously considered to be nothing but a ring of adversaries. Then he was on his feet, glaring down at her like an angry Titan. "I've had enough of your commission, enough of your accusations, and Miss Ryan, I've had enough of you!"

Jonnie forced herself to remain calm as Dan stormed from the room, leaving behind a stunned silence. Gradually the haunting stillness cracked, replaced by the buzz of startled conversation.

"I'd like next to call Mrs. Ann Bishop," Jonnie said, raising her voice to be heard above the din.

Chapter Fourteen

Ann Bishop twisted her hands together in her lap, casting worried looks in the direction of her husband, seated across the room. Brian's drawn face offered encouragement.

"I told Coach Kincade I wanted to come forward," she offered in a soft, unhappy voice, twisting a strand of dark chestnut hair in her fingers. "Brian told him, too, when you first came to Cascades, Miss Ryan. But he wouldn't allow it. He kept saying he'd handle everything his own way."

She shook her head, and Jonnie identified with her frustration. Dan had accused her of being intransigent. But he could make the rock of Gibraltar look like a mere pebble. She knew that once he'd made up his mind, Ann and Brian and all the king's men couldn't have changed it.

Jonnie knew the story was a difficult one for Ann to tell. Both she and her husband had been defensive when Jonnie had shown up on their doorstep late last night in the pouring rain. But by the time she'd left the Bishop home, the three had been united in their goal to get Dan off the hook. Which wasn't going to be easy, Jonnie considered, since the dummy was making it look as if he'd committed grand larceny.

"When Dan first gave us the money," Ann continued slowly, "we never realized it was against the rules."

A murmur broke out among the listeners, and Jonnie hastened to dispel their obvious skepticism. Out of the corner of her eye she viewed William leaning forward in his chair and knew she'd have to tread softly. It was too early to tip her hand.

"That's a bit difficult to believe, Mrs. Bishop. Surely you and your husband understood the rules."

"We knew we weren't allowed to keep any money," Ann allowed. "But this is a loan. I brought the papers with me to prove it." She handed them to Jonnie, who in turn handed them to the court official who was acting as bailiff in the hearings.

"According to the rule book, loans are outside the perimeters," Jonnie explained to Ann, as well as the listeners in the hearing room. "All too often they are conveniently forgotten, or forgiven. In that instance, the loan becomes nothing but a paperwork loophole for payoffs."

Jonnie slid a surreptitious glance toward William, watching as he leaned back in his chair with satisfaction. She knew he was envisioning the noose slipping over Dan's head.

"That's not how it was." Ann's eyes were dark with sorrow as she took a deep breath and turned toward Jonnie. "I want to explain. But first, may I make a personal observation?"

William stiffened, and Jonnie held her breath, waiting for his objection. She instinctively sensed that he would choose to avoid a public debate with his own appointee, and she was proven right as he held his tongue. However, his fingers were gripping both ends of a pencil as if he wished he could wrap them about Jonnie's neck.

Ann's voice was soft, but succeeded in capturing the attention of everyone in the room as she leaned forward, stressing her point.

"Your investigation has been all facts and figures; you never asked anything important. You only wanted to know how much the scholarships were for, who paid the plane tickets out to visit the campus, did the players fly first class or coach?"

Her hazel eyes were faintly accusing, even now that she knew Jonnie's attitude had changed. "Everyone answered your questions, hoping you'd let them tell you something about Coach Kincade. But there's something a lot more important than all your ledger sheets and statistics. You can't investigate an athletic program without looking at the man running the show, Miss Ryan. And you refused to do that.

"You have to understand, the athlete is not part of the student population. There's no way he fits into the mainstream of college life. A team player becomes a species apart—he eats, lives, sleeps, breathes for four years with his own kind. If he hasn't already figured it out before he arrives on campus, pretty soon he wakes up one morning and realizes he's more athlete than student.''

Jonnie listened to the explanation, knowing that while she'd always watched her father and her brothers, she'd never understood how far removed their lives had been from that of the general college population.

"It's a hard life. The athlete spends too much time injured, and he's chronically tired, especially if he's one of those trying to balance the two lives into some semblance of a united whole, like my husband was doing. Brian traveled almost as much as the pros, but at the same time his classes were horribly disrupted. For those players, like Brian, who are married, it's even more of a merry-go-round.''

Ann turned to her husband as if for support to continue, and the fond look he bestowed upon his wife indicated Brian Bishop would not have foregone that part of his grueling existence for a moment.

"What frustrated all of us about you, Miss Ryan, was that you never wanted to listen to the important stuff. When you're isolated like a college athlete is, the coach takes on added importance. He's got the ability to steer lives in whatever direction he's decided is important.

"Coach Kincade is tough. His discipline is rigid. There are no privileges, no excuses to get out of anything. But everyone knows he's that way because he cares. He cares about the players as individuals, cares about them being educated as well as being able to play ball, and he cares about the contribution each of them can make toward society. That's what you should have put in your report.''

There was a long, thoughtful silence in the room as Ann paused for breath and Jonnie considered the case of the apocryphal university president who was asked which he believed to be the major problem with the uneducated athlete at the administrative level—ignorance or apathy.

"I don't know and I don't care," he'd replied.

She sighed, thinking the story not very funny since it was so true.

Calvin Dunn had attempted to show her that Dan and Cascades were an exception, but she'd only seen it as an interesting story of a player who'd used basketball as a way out of the ghetto. She hadn't paid enough attention to the fact that Dan had shown him a permanent way out. She'd been so concerned with collecting data, it was no wonder Dan had doubted that she even had a heart.

"That's what we're here for today, Ann. We're trying to understand. Tell me about the loans," she requested softly.

A sharp sound shattered the silence as the yellow pencil snapped in William's hands.

"Brian had just made the Academic All-American team. We were going out for a celebration dinner when we were hit by a drunk driver. The accident destroyed cells in the left side of my brain which control muscle function. I was left what they call a hemiplegic. We didn't think I'd ever walk again.''

Her reminiscent smile was weak, but it managed to brighten up the young woman's face. ''Dan had read about some experimental surgery being done at Loyola and encouraged us to try to get admitted to the program. There was only one problem.''

''The money,'' offered Jonnie.

''Since the technique is still in the pioneering stages, they were happy to find someone who met all their qualifications. The procedure only works on about ten percent of hemiplegics, and I fit their profile perfectly. The surgery team agreed to donate their time, and Loyola was willing to absorb the cost of the medical center. But there were travel expenses and living expenses while I received the follow-up therapy. We don't have any money.

''The only reason Brian is on the team,'' Ann explained, ''was because the athletic scholarship was so generous. It paid for everything and enabled him to put himself through school and allowed us to get married, too. Of course, I worked up until the accident. And I'll be able to return to work soon. I've regained nearly eighty percent of the use of my legs—far beyond the doctors' wildest expectations. The surgery opened a closed door.

''But without the loans, Brian would've been forced to drop out of school and work full time. And I don't know what would have happened to me.''

"So you'll soon begin paying off the loan." Jonnie's tone was gentle, encouraging.

Leading the witness, she offered a silent objection to her own tactics. But not one attentive individual moved to stop her. She knew William was dying to, but it was too late. The consummate politician was discovering he'd made the first tactical error of a brilliant career.

Ann nodded decisively. "That's right. And Brian's been offered a teaching position in Portland, so we've figured out a schedule that allows us to repay Coach Kincade within the next three years."

The soft voice of Ann Bishop had captured the attention of the entire room as she'd slowly, painfully, related her story in detail. Jonnie allowed the silence to linger for a long moment, savoring the rapt, sympathetic expressions on everyone's face. Everyone's but the smoldering countenance of William Murdock.

The young woman's hazel eyes glistened with tears as they moved past Jonnie to the hushed, attentive jury. "Although we'll never be able to pay him back for everything he's done for me. And for our life together."

Ann's eyes returned to Jonnie. "If you're going to find the man guilty, Miss Ryan, you're going to have to find him guilty of caring too much."

Jonnie felt the lump blocking her throat, and this time her silence was not staged.

"Thank you, Mrs. Bishop," she managed to say finally. "No more questions."

"You realize you're finished, don't you?" William's eyes burned her skin as Jonnie returned to the table, scorching her with undisguised hatred. "Washed up. Kaput. Done."

"I know all the words, William," she answered weakly, feeling her bones turn to water. "I always got A's in creative writing."

There was a startled, collective cry from the spectators as Jonnie slid forward in her chair, ending up on the floor in a loose-limbed heap.

"You're crazy, do you know that?"

At the beautifully familiar voice, Jonnie forced her eyes open to find Dan Kincade standing next to her bed, his eyes filled with a look that was half-loving and half-admonishing.

"I know. You used to tell me that enough times when I was a kid," she mumbled, her mouth feeling as if it was stuffed with cotton batting. "You never did approve of my methods."

"Here."

Dan extended the water glass toward her, one strong arm moving under her head to lift her so she could take sips of the tepid water.

"The two have nothing to do with each other. While you're still crazier than a bedbug, Jonnie Ryan, and totally uncontrollable, I approve of you wholeheartedly."

"I learned about your rules, Dan. I want you to know that."

He laughed a deep, happy sound. It had been so long since she'd heard that uncensored sound of the man enjoying himself. Jonnie decided that a steady dose of it would certainly cure her faster than any antibiotic.

"Sweetheart, while you've been lying here, worrying us half to death and adding innumerable gray hairs to your poor father's head, the entire state discovered exactly what you did with the rules. And after the wire service picked up the reports of your little grandstand play, the rest of the nation did too."

"What happened?"

"I'm not saying there aren't going to be repercussions. In fact, for a time it looked as if I might be out of a job. But, E.G. Harrison and the board of regents aren't as independent-thinking as a certain gutsy investigator I know. . . .

"When the phone started ringing off the hook and the telegrams and letters started pouring in, they decided I'd make a pretty unpopular sacrificial lamb." He grinned. "You not only managed to save my hide, but you single-handedly created absolute chaos in the higher echelons of collegiate sports."

Dan's grin widened, the broad white crescent brightening his face with distinct pleasure. "It's coming as a discomforting thought to some people that you can't go through life wearing blinders. You've given everyone concerned with the problem a good start on ulcers as they scramble to come up with some guidelines allowing for leeway on an individual basis."

Jonnie closed her eyes for a moment, her legal mind turning over the problem she knew would prove a difficult one. She'd certainly spent enough time wrestling with it lately. One would have to be a Solomon to consider each case on a truly individual basis.

"I've really opened Pandora's box this time, haven't I, Dan?"

His cool hand brushed the fiery auburn hair from her forehead before his lips left a light kiss there. "That you have, love, that you have."

Jonnie's somber gaze caught his, seeking reassurance that it would, in the end, all turn out to be worth it. "In the meantime, what will happen?"

"In the meantime, honey, good people will do what they've always done. They'll attempt to get through life following their consciences as best they can.

"Speaking of which," he continued, "it's taken all five Ryans to keep track of the messages waiting for you. You seem to be in demand these days, counselor. I suppose we'll have to add Joan of Arc to Wonder Woman, Eleanor Roosevelt and Morgan Fairchild. It must be getting crowded in that luscious female body."

"What kinds of messages?"

"Oh, you know—the usual. All sorts of people wanting you to take on cases for them. Cleaning up waste dumps, filing suits against discriminatory employers, one guy can't get his neighbor's dog to stop barking at three in the morning...just your usual white knight sort of stuff."

Jonnie considered his words for a moment. "That's something I'm going to have to think about—going into private practice. The party will probably revoke my registration."

Dan's eyes were laced with tender censorship. "Just because you've found out the world isn't perfect, honey, don't go off the deep end. Half the messages are from the party, asking you to stay on."

"Stay? On the Murdock Commission? After what I did?" Jonnie couldn't believe it.

She wasn't surprised when Dan shook his head in the negative. But his next words stunned her.

"Uh-uh. Heading up the Ryan Commission looking into ways to make the collegiate athletic system more manageable."

Jonnie shook her head, deciding it was far too much to consider at this time. She'd think about it later. Right now she only wanted to revel in the fact that it was over—and that Dan was here with her.

"Your poor, dear beautiful eye. I'm sorry Jason hit you." She lifted her hand to lightly touch the swollen skin that had blossomed into a brilliant green and yellow ringing his eye.

"Somebody had to knock some sense into me."

"Did you hit him back?" she asked, realizing that Jason had never shown any indications of being in a struggle, other than his skinned hand.

"Are you kidding? There were three very good reasons why I couldn't do that."

Jonnie trailed a gentle finger down the side of his smiling face.

"And what were those?"

"In the first place, Jason is bigger than me. Hell, Jason is bigger than anyone I know." Dan laughed, and Jonnie lightly joined in. "Secondly, I knew I deserved it for the way I'd been treating you. And third, he's my girl's brother. It just didn't seem proper, somehow."

"I love you," she breathed, tracing the full line of his lips, her fingertip dipping into the deep cleft on his chin.

"I know. You've given me that gift twice before," Dan replied, his blue eyes warm and tender as they caressed her face. "I'd say it's about time I took you up on it. Before you decide to throw in the towel and take your love elsewhere."

"Never." A puzzled frown skittered across her brow as his words sank in. "Twice?"

"Twice." Dan nodded and Jonnie knew she'd never tire of watching those lovely jet curls dance on his dark forehead. "The second time was in Denver."

Jonnie rubbed at her temple with her fingertips, trying to smooth away the headache the effort to think was creating.

"I don't remember."

"I didn't think you realized you'd said it. You were sick, and I think it just slipped out. I didn't say anything about it at the time, because quite honestly, babe, I hadn't wanted to hear it."

"Because of the commission?"

"That." Dan laced their fingers together, lifting her hand to his lips. "And the fact I was still having problems separating the sexy lady from the cute kid."

"And now?" she inquired softly.

"And now I suppose it's high time I admitted to my sweet, brave lady exactly how much I love her. I do, you know."

Jonnie rewarded the slightly tentative confession with a blissful smile. "I know, Dan. I've known for a long time, but I was beginning to worry that I'd never hear you say it."

"Get used to it, sweetheart. Because I intend to spend the rest of my life reminding you that I love you, just in case you're tempted to forget."

"Never." Her eyelids were growing heavy, and she struggled to keep Dan's smiling face in focus.

His tender expression grew stern. "And now it's time for you to get to sleep. I'm having a hard time keeping myself from sharing that bed with you. You've gotten under my skin, Jonnie Ryan. Freckles and all."

"I'm so glad," she murmured sleepily, her hand still wrapped in his as she pressed it to her breast.

"Roll over. You're going to get sunburned."

"No, I'm not. I'm fine. Besides, Daniel Kincade, rolling over takes far too much energy."

Jonnie squeezed her eyes shut against the blazing ball of Hawaiian sun. The heat was a glorious thing, warming her bones, drying out the moisture that seemed to have seeped into them from the wet Willamette winter.

"God, you are stubborn! And just as argumentative as ever," Dan complained lightly, taking her in his arms and flipping her as easily as a pancake on a grill. "I thought marriage was supposed to mellow a woman, settle her down."

He knelt on the blanket they'd spread on the sand, straddling her outstretched legs as he began to massage the suntan oil into the skin of her back.

"Ummm." Jonnie moved under his sensuous touch like a cat basking in a sunbeam. "I think you're melting me. And for your information, although it's one more thing I never learned at a mother's knee, I think that old wives' tale refers to dogs." She sighed deeply, loving the touch of his hands on her body.

"It's just as well," he growled playfully, leaning down to nip lightly at the lobe of her ear, "I prefer you on the wild side." His crisp chest hairs brushed against her oiled back, bringing a flood of tactile sensations rushing to her languid mind.

"I'm glad you're satisfied, Mr. Kincade. I do so aim to please."

"I'm pleased, all right, Mrs. Kincade. But far from satisfied," he promised.

"Did you see Judge Warner and his wife at the reception?" she murmured, loving the minstrations of his strong hands. "I wonder if we'll still look that much in love forty-five years from now."

"Although I know I'll love you a hundred years from now, sweetheart, I've told you every time you've brought it up that I didn't see a single soul at that party except you. I couldn't get over how beautiful you looked in that dress.''

"If you liked it so much, you shouldn't have been in such a hurry to get it off," she teased, turning her head to grin up at him. "But really, Dan, he couldn't keep his eyes off her. You'd think it was *their* wedding."

"You're a card-carrying romantic, Jonnie. I knew it from the start." Dan's palms moved down the back of her legs, his thumbs rubbing the soft spot behind her knees.

"And you're a cynic,". she retorted lightly, refusing to be dissuaded from her romantic illusions. She couldn't remember ever being as happy as she'd been the past two weeks. "It was nice of the judge to let us use this house for our honeymoon, don't you think? It's so beautiful. And a private beach—absolutely heaven."

"Nice." His hands were concentrating on her firm thighs, massaging with strong, sensuous strokes. "And the privacy is by far the nicest part."

"Agreed. And speaking of that. . . ." Jonnie's silky laugh was a silver-edged invitation as she sat up, moving her hands to his wide shoulders, pressing him back down onto the blanket.

"You realize of course, woman, that continuing such behavior could result in you ending up with sand in the most unusual places."

"That's what the blanket is for," she grinned. "Besides, I'm willing to risk it, if you are," she murmured provocatively, kissing his smiling mouth. Jonnie continued her teasing torment, her fingers dancing like graceful sea birds over his deeply tanned male flesh.

"Stop that, wanton," he complained laughingly. "My God, woman, don't you ever get enough?

"You've spent a lot of your life chasing after me," Dan teased on a muffled groan as her fingernail flicked against a taut male nipple. "Did you ever feel I might not be worth it?"

"What do you think?" Jonnie folded her hands on his chest and propped her chin on them, fixing him with a bright, teasing gaze. "The only problem now is, what am I going to do with you?"

Dan pulled her slick, pliant body against him. A slow, wicked grin spread across his face, and in the bright tropical sunlight his eyes glowed with promise and love. "Don't worry, sweetheart," he murmured. "Your husband will think of something."

And he did—lovingly, passionately, tenderly—again and again.

Bestselling Author

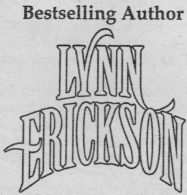

Dares you to enter a wonderland of passion and sin in

Meet the Connellys:

Matt—the charismatic, scandal-ridden senator determined to hide the truth.

Lee—the wife who drowns her sorrows in the bottle.

Terry—the prodigal son, who always gets what he wants, at all costs.

Beth—the jet-setting daughter who can no longer run from the past or her family.

And the one man who can bring it all tumbling down—
Case McCandless, town sheriff sworn to ferret out the truth, and destined to find love with the enemy.

Take 3 of "The Best of the Best™" Novels FREE

Plus get a FREE surprise gift!

New York Times Bestselling Author

BARBARA DELINSKY

What do you call a man who flits from woman to woman?

CARDINAL RULES

Corey Haraden is a wealthy man-about-town known affectionately by his friends as the "Cardinal." That is until he meets a very serious and aloof market analyst named Corinne Fremont. Sparks fly and, determined to push things further, Corey hires her to do some tourist research for his hotel chain. Before long, business becomes pleasure. Now it's up to Corinne. Can she forget her past fears and abandon herself to passion? The only problem is that within Corey's strong embrace, Corinne's heart has a mind of its own.

Available this August
wherever MIRA Books are sold.

MIRA The brightest star in women's fiction

MBD3

Twelve-time *New York Times* bestselling author

This August experience an unforgettable story with

Theresa Brubaker was as innocent as she was unsure. Brian Scanlon was a proud, sensitive man whose feelings of betrayal ran deep.

Now, a bold decision she made alone threatens to destroy their love. Join Theresa and Brian as they find out if love really does conquer all.

Available wherever books are sold.

If you love the intriguing tales of

JoANN ROSS

Act now to order another passionate story
by one of MIRA's exceptional authors:

#66018	LEGACY OF LIES	$4.99 U.S. ☐
		$5.50 CAN. ☐
#66022	DUSK FIRE	$4.99 U.S. ☐
		$5.50 CAN. ☐

(limited quantities available)

TOTAL AMOUNT $
POSTAGE & HANDLING $
($1.00 for one book, 50¢ for each additional)
APPLICABLE TAXES* $ _____
TOTAL PAYABLE $ _____
(check or money order—please do not send cash)

To order, complete this form and send it, along with a check or money
order for the total above, payable to MIRA Books, to: **In the U.S.:** 3010
Walden Avenue, P.O. Box 9077, Buffalo, NY 14269-9077; **In Canada:** P.O.
Box 636, Fort Erie, Ontario, L2A 5X3.

Name: _____
Address: _____ City: _____
State/Prov.: _____ Zip/Postal Code: _____

*New York residents remit applicable sales taxes.
 Canadian residents remit applicable GST and provincial taxes.   MJRBL2

MIRA